REMEMBER MY LOVE

Pamela Macaluso

A KISMET™ Romance

METEOR PUBLISHING CORPORATION
Bensalem, Pennsylvania

KISMET™ is a trademark of Meteor Publishing Corporation

Copyright © 1990 Pamela Macaluso
Cover Art copyright © 1990 Michael R. Powell

All rights reserved.

No part of this book may be reproduced, stored in a retrieval system, or transmitted in any form, by any means, including mechanical, electronic, photocopying, recording or otherwise, without prior written permission of the publisher, Meteor Publishing Corporation, 3369 Progress Drive, Bensalem, PA 19020.

First Printing December 1990.

ISBN: 1-878702-23-8

All the characters in this book are fictitious. Any resemblance to actual persons, living or dead, is purely coincidental.

Printed in the United States of America

For Joseph

Many thanks for the most romantic anniversary gift of all—an electric typewriter!

PAMELA MACALUSO

Pamela Macaluso has traveled through or lived in most areas of the United States. She has found a wealth of romantic settings to inspire her writing—including Montana and her native California. Home is now Florida's Space Coast, with her husband and their two sons. A former math instructor, she is now following a long-time dream of being a writer.

ONE

"That's him, Dr. Sheridan." Deanna Palmer looked across the sunny hospital lounge, noting every detail of the man before her. She mentally compared what she saw to the photographic image she had become so familiar with over the last week.

Without a doubt this was Maxwell Hilliard. Thirty-six, six feet tall, medium-brown hair, blue-gray eyes . . . There was something different about his eyes. The eyes she'd been looking for were cold and hard. The eyes that looked up to meet her gaze were laughing, smiling eyes with a glint of mischief.

"Mac," the doctor beside her called out. "Can I speak to you a minute?"

"Mac?" Deanna questioned Dr. Sheridan as Max put down the cards he was holding, excused himself from his three companions, and headed across the room.

"We had to call him something after we found out that he wasn't Adam Hunter, although that was the name he'd used to lease the truck. He didn't care for John Doe, so he came up with Mac. It stands for Master at Cards—MAC."

"He certainly didn't lose his sense of humor when he lost his memory."

"What can I do for you, Doc?" Max asked as he reached them. His words were for Dr. Sheridan, but his attention was focused on Deanna. His eyes swept over her, not missing a single inch. He started at the top of her head, past her long, flowing chestnut hair. He made a quick appraisal of her face, the worried green eyes watching him. He continued his inspection of her feminine curves and ended at her small feet that were hidden away inside snowboots. "Have we met before? I feel like I know you from somewhere."

Dr. Sheridan looked pleased. "This is Mrs. Palmer, Mac. Does the name mean anything to you?"

"No." Max looked deep into Deanna's eyes. She felt as though he were probing into the depths of her soul. "I *do* know you from somewhere."

Deanna was speechless. Max's reaction to her was just what she needed to convince Dr. Sheridan that the man he thought of as Mac was her husband. Earlier Dr. Sheridan had told her that some amnesia patients recognized the important people from their lives without remembering who they were. It was helpful that he claimed to remember her, but it was very unsettling, for she and Maxwell Hilliard had never met. Her instincts told her to run, but she had a job to do.

"Kevin," she cried, managing a break in her voice as she threw herself into Max's arms. "I've been so worried."

Max returned her embrace, holding her close against him. Deanna felt the strong muscles of his chest and heard the rapid beating of his heart. His shoulders curled forward to enfold her in a warm, safe cocoon.

She had forgotten how good it felt to be held in rugged, masculine arms and was reluctant to end the contact. After a few moments, she pulled back and looked up at him.

He smiled down at her. His attention shifted to her lips. "I have a strong urge to kiss you, but before I do . . . what's our relationship? Are you my sister, girlfriend . . . lover?"

"Ah . . ." Deanna began. The blood rushed to her cheeks. Her eyes dropped to his full, sensuous mouth that seemed to be at odds with his strong, determined jaw.

"She's your wife," Dr. Sheridan answered for her.

"Good," Max murmured softly before his mouth

came down on hers with all the passion expected from two separated lovers.

Deanna was stunned. It had been a long time since she had been kissed, and she could honestly say that she'd *never* been kissed quite like this before. She let herself be swept up in the magic he was weaving around her as he moved his mouth seductively over hers.

The sound of clapping and whistling pierced the fog in Deanna's mind. The card players and other occupants of the lounge were saluting their reunion. Deanna pulled away from Max.

If that was a sample of his expertise as a lover, he well deserved his reputation, she thought to herself. She found herself wondering what it would be like to really be married to this man.

But for now, she had to think of Max as her husband until she had him safely turned over to his father. "May we go now, Dr. Sheridan?" she asked.

"Yes. Mac . . . er . . . Kevin, why don't you go back to your room and dress. Mrs. Palmer brought a suitcase with some of your clothes. Meet us in my office when you're ready."

"Right." After a quick kiss for Deanna, Max headed down the hallway.

Deanna and Dr. Sheridan returned to his office. "Let me stress again, our staff agrees that your husband's condition is most likely temporary, caused by the blow to his head in the accident. We feel that when all the swelling has gone down, his memory will return. If you'll give me the name and address of your doctor, I will send him the medical records of your husband's stay here."

"My father-in-law has contacted a Dr. Fletcher." She pulled out a three-by-five card with the doctor's address and phone number and gave it to Dr. Sheridan. "Before you mail the records, may I use your phone to call my father-in-law. He was trying to arrange things so that Dr. Fletcher would meet us up here."

"Certainly." He set the phone on the front of his desk.

Deanna dialed Alexander Hilliard's unlisted personal phone number.

"Hello."

"This is Deanna. It's him."

"Excellent! Any problems?" Deanna could hear the smile in his voice.

"Other than the amnesia, no. The doctor says he has some minor cuts and bruises, but they're healing well."

"Is he willing to leave with you?"

"Yes." Very willing, she thought.

"Good, take him back to the cabin. I'll get in touch with Dr. Fletcher and we'll join you there."

"All right. Dr. Sheridan has medical records here at the hospital for Dr. Fletcher."

"He'll probably want to speak to Dr. Sheridan, as well. I'll pass on the message to him. We'll see you soon."

"Good-bye." She hung up the phone. "Dr. Fletcher will be coming here."

"Fine. I'll keep the records for him." Dr. Sheridan picked up the driver's license, marriage license, and wedding photo that Deanna had brought with her as identification to have Max released. After glancing at them again, he put them back into the envelope and handed them to her. "Will you be staying with friends in the area?"

"Friends of ours have a cabin near Monarch. We'll be staying there." She nervously turned the heavy gold band around on her finger. It felt strange to be wearing it again after two years without it.

"Why don't you jot down the address and phone number for me in case I need to get in touch with you. And feel free to contact me if there's anything I can do for you." He handed Deanna a pen and pad of paper. She wrote down the address and phone number of Max's cabin.

As she handed the pad back to Dr. Sheridan, Max came in, followed by a fellow patient. "So this is the little woman, eh?" He smiled at Deanna. "News travels fast in this place. Everyone's pleased that Mac found his identity, but there's more than one disappointed female now that they know he's married."

"That's understandable," Deanna replied as her gaze swept over the tall, handsome man by her side.

Good-byes and well wishes were exchanged all around. Deanna soon found herself sitting behind the wheel of her rental car with Maxwell Hilliard by her side. The search was over.

It had begun a week before when her brother had called her into his office.

Gordon Kane, head of Kane Investigations, sat behind his desk, the sunlight streaming in through the window behind him. His hair had less red than Deanna's and his eyes were blue, while hers were green. He was thirty-two, four years older than Deanna's twenty-eight.

Deanna sensed something was wrong when Gordon waved her distractedly into a chair without his usual greeting of a brotherly hug and kiss.

"I just had a call from Alexander Hilliard."

"Was something wrong with the jewels you recovered?"

"No . . . no, the jewels were all right and are now safely guarded by his new state-of-the-art security system." Gordon tapped the end of his pencil against the notepad on his desk. "His son is missing."

"Kidnapped?"

"He doesn't think so. They argued and Max stormed off."

"Why doesn't Mr. Hilliard call his son's friends, check the resort areas? Surely his own staff can handle this without the need for a private investigator."

"The problem is that the investigation has to be very discreet. They have a big contract coming up.

Max's signature is essential. If word gets out that he's missing, the whole deal might fall apart."

"He's probably planning a last-minute grand entrance, Gordon. From what I've heard of the man, it sounds like his style."

"That's what Mr. Hilliard thought, too. But the signing was to have been this morning and Max didn't show up. Mr. Hilliard has gained a month's extension using legal technicalities, but he's got to find Max."

"So, who have you assigned to the case, and what kind of information do they want me to acquire for them?" Deanna reached out and took a pad of paper and a pencil from Gordon's desk.

"Actually, Deanna, I was hoping you would consider taking it."

"Me? Gordon, I'm not a detective. I'm a research assistant, remember?"

"I know, but because of the highly secret nature of this case and the fact that it's for Alex Hilliard, I can't trust it to just anyone. I'd do it myself, but I've become too well known with all the publicity of finding Mr. Hilliard's jewels and breaking that drug ring the month before. You're sharp, intuitive, have a definite knack for ferreting out information and I'd make you an investigator in a minute if—"

"Gordon, I will not carry a gun."

"All right, I won't start that again. But what about helping with the Hilliard case?"

Deanna sighed. "I'll give it a try."

"Keep in mind, you can't run around town flashing his picture, asking if anyone's seen him or call any of his friends and ask if they know his whereabouts. You'll have to use roundabout methods. You have an appointment with Alexander Hilliard at one o'clock." Gordon gave her a three-by-five card with a Bel Air address.

"Wish me luck." Deanna stood up and smoothed a hand down her gray wool skirt.

"Don't forget, this is completely confidential. I don't even want the rest of the agency to know what you're working on."

Deanna spent the rest of the morning compiling a profile sketch of Maxwell Hilliard—major stockholder and heir to Hilliard, Branson, and Hilliard, the investment firm started by his father and his mother's brother. Max was an only child, and since his uncle's marriage produced no children, the entire empire would one day be his alone.

From all accounts he worked hard and had earned the right to have his name on the company letterhead. It was also common knowledge that he played as hard as he worked. His name had been linked with a long list of women: actresses, models, a female race-car driver—the list was endless. He'd even had a prominent feminist publicly vow that she'd give up her career and stay home if Max would come home to her every night.

Deanna arrived early for her appointment with Alex Hilliard, but was shown in immediately. The study was a blend of functional and comfortable. With its polished wood paneling and leather furniture, it looked like a room right out of an English country estate. Alex was sitting behind his desk with a stack of papers in front of him, but his attention was focused out the large diamond-paned window to his left. His forehead was creased in deep thought, his eyes troubled.

"Ms. Palmer is here, sir." At the sound of the servant's voice, Alex stood.

"Ms. Palmer, thank you for coming. Mrs. Nolan, bring us some coffee, please. Unless you'd prefer tea or a soft drink?" he asked Deanna.

"No, coffee is fine."

"Sit down," Alex gestured to the chair before his desk after Mrs. Nolan had left the room. When they were both seated, he continued. "I've gathered up some information that you might find helpful and I'm ready to answer any questions you may have." He handed her a file folder.

Deanna took her pen from her purse. Sitting forward in her chair, she asked, "Since speaking with Mr. Kane you haven't received any phone calls or letters suggesting that this might be a kidnapping?"

"No."

"When did you last see your son?"

"Last Wednesday, a week ago today. I wasn't worried at first. We had argued . . ." His voice faded away as he stared thoughtfully at the ceiling.

"What was the argument about?"

"Max has been putting together a project for a resort hotel chain. He's lined up a number of investors but plans on using a large portion of Hilliard, Branson, and Hilliard funds as well. Personally, I oppose the project and I told him so." Alex ran his hands through his hair. "Despite my advice, he went ahead with his plans. He presented his ideas to the board, and in spite of my objections, he won the vote."

Deanna could see where that would lead to an argument. Alex Hilliard was a proud, determined man, and she was sure he didn't enjoy losing any battle.

A soft knock on the door preceded Mrs. Nolan's entrance with their coffee. She had also included a plate of cookies on the tray. After fixing each of them a cup of coffee, Mrs. Nolan left them alone once again.

"All of Max's investors arrived this morning to finalize the arrangements, but Max didn't show up."

"Could he have changed his mind and decided to abandon the project as a peace offering to you?"

"If he had, he would have told me his decision in person or at the very least have contacted the investors and told them not to come. Something has to be wrong. I would look for him myself or have my security department on the case, but if word got back to any of the investors it could jeopardize Max's project."

"A project that you'd just as soon see scrapped."

"Very true, but Max won his victory fairly, and I will do all in my power to help him succeed." He sighed. "Even wining and dining his investors when I'd rather be looking for him."

By the time Deanna left she had a wealth of information on Maxwell Hilliard, as well as an eight-by-ten photograph. There was no denying that the man was attractive. Deanna noticed a strong resemblance to his father. She propped the picture up on her bedroom dresser. It was the last thing she saw every night and the first thing she saw every morning.

She spent her days gathering information, and in the evenings she would sort through it. Cold blue-gray eyes watched her from her dresser. Despite Alex's feelings to the contrary, Deanna thought that Max was deliberately staying away. According to the information she had gathered about him, it sounded like something he would do. He had a reputation for being ruthless and heartless. She wondered how a warm, caring man like Alex Hilliard could have ended up with a son like Max.

"You know, Mr. Hilliard," Deanna laughed to herself. "I'll bet your ego could fill the Grand Canyon. I wonder how you'll react when you realize you've lost your game of hide-and-seek? I'm going to find you, Mr. Hilliard—you can count on it."

As the days went by, Deanna found herself talking more and more to the photo. She even slipped into the habit of calling him Max, instead of Mr. Hilliard.

Six days after Gordon had first assigned her to the case, she was back in his office.

"Gordon, I need to go to Montana."

"Montana? Maxwell Hilliard is in Montana?" Gordon's eyes widened in disbelief.

"I'm almost positive that he is."

"What has led you to this conclusion?"

"Thorough researching with a large dose of sheer luck."

Gordon laughed. "That's the magic recipe."

"At first I hit a lot of dead ends. All of his cars, his plane, and boat were accounted for. His luggage was in his closet. There was no record of a taxi coming to the house. No airplane, train, or bus tickets charged on his credit cards—in fact, nothing at all on the cards or out of his personal bank accounts since his disappearance."

"Wouldn't it be logical to assume then that he is still in the city?"

Deanna nodded. "I checked out all the obvious hiding places."

"Including Jennifer Brady?" Gordon named the actress who was Max's most recent love interest.

"Yes, Gordon, I visited Miss Brady. I pretended to be a free-lance writer hoping to get my big break by writing an article about her. Miss Brady quickly changed the subject when I brought up their relationship. I was later able to find out from the housekeeper that Max missed a date they had scheduled for the night he disappeared. He hasn't contacted her since."

"The man must be crazy—standing up Jennifer Brady!"

"Maybe you should go over and try to console her."

Gordon leaned back in his chair, hands behind his head. "I just might do that."

Deanna moved the conversation back to Max. "I was pretending to be a scorned lover trying to get information out of the staff at his various houses and apartments to see if he was in residence when the police called Mr. Hilliard to report that Max's bicycle had been found at the airport. A man who works for a car-rental agency noticed that the bike was there day in and day out. He reported it to the security guards and they called the police. Since the license was current they called the Hilliards to see if the bike had been stolen recently." Deanna looked over at her brother, who was still gazing dreamily at the ceiling. "Earth to Gordon. Come in, Gordon."

"Keep going, I'm listening."

"What was the last thing I said?"

"Earth to Gordon. Come in, Gordon." He flashed her a smile.

"Let me know if they legalize fratricide," she teased. "I meant before that."

"Before that, you were saying that the police had contacted the Hilliards to see if they'd had a bicycle stolen."

"Amazing."

"Never underestimate me, sister dear. Continue."

"Since the bike was at the airport, I started going through the passenger lists looking for cash transactions."

"The airlines cooperated?"

"Well . . . no," Deanna hedged.

"Charlie?"

"Charlie." Deanna confessed to the identity of her accomplice.

"I bought you that computer to store your research and keep track of our closed cases."

"But it's capable of so much more than that."

"The legality of some of which is still in question."

"Regardless, Charlie got me the names of cash customers without prior reservations for the twenty-four-hour period following Max's disappearance. There weren't many. Most people make reservations ahead of time and pay with credit cards or a check."

"He may have cards and checks in another name."

"I realize that, but fortunately, while I was checking the list Charlie gave me, I found a man who checked in no luggage and whose alleged address is occupied by a family named Bigelow. None of them have ever heard of Adam Hunter. Also the post office had no record of Mr. Hunter ever having lived there."

"Could be our Mr. Hilliard. Where did he go?"

"He flew to Denver and then up to Great Falls, Montana."

"Not exactly a Club Med vacation spot."

"No, but the list of Max's houses and apartments included a cabin in the Little Belt Mountains, about sixty miles from Great Falls."

"Sounds good to me. You're a credit to the agency and the family tree."

"There's just one catch." Deanna hated to take the wind out of Gordon's sails, but she had no choice. "In Great Falls, Adam Hunter rented a four-wheel drive truck. Somehow he bought or charmed his way past the major credit card requirement and I.D. check or has them in the name Adam Hunter. The truck was returned to the rental company the next day by the Highway Patrol. There'd been an accident—"

"Oh, God," Gordon cut her off. "How is he?"

"Adam Hunter is alive and physically well in a hospital in Great Falls."

"Good. Go get him."

"The problem is, he's lost his memory."

"Run that by me again, please."

"He's lost his memory. He doesn't know who he is. He had no identification with him when they brought him in. It was either lost at the scene of the accident or he'd left it at the cabin. If—and there is still an *if* here—if Adam Hunter is Maxwell Hilliard."

"There's only one way to find out. Go home and pack."

"I need a few things from you first." Deanna took out her list. "I talked to a Dr. Sheridan at the hospital. Adam Hunter seems to fit the description of Max. If it is Max, I'll need some form of identification for him, and some form of identification to prove our relationship to each other . . . maybe a note from Mr. Hilliard authorizing them to release Max to me?"

"You didn't give them Max's name, did you?"

"No, I just gave them mine, asked for a description of Adam Hunter, and told them that I'd be there as soon as possible."

Gordon sat quietly staring into space. "Do you still have a copy of your marriage license?"

"Yes. Why?"

"We're going to have Max released in Kevin's name to avoid publicity. Bring your marriage license and stop by the office in three hours. Then be on the next plane to Great Falls."

The manila envelope she'd picked up from Gordon now sat on the car dashboard. Max picked it up. Inside was the copy of her marriage license—a marriage that had lasted eighteen months and had been over for two years now. There was a California driver's license in the name of Kevin Palmer with Max's picture and description on it. There was also a color wedding portrait. The agency's photographer had substituted Max's face for Kevin's. He'd done such a good job that she had trouble remembering what the original picture had looked like.

"We make a nice-looking couple." Max was looking intently at the photo. "I just wish to God I could remember our wedding." He raked his free hand through his hair. "Such a beautiful bride."

He continued to study their likenesses as Deanna left town heading east on Highway 89. She was astonished by how quickly civilization ended and the great white wilderness stretched before them. It had snowed the week before, but the weather today was clear, and the blue skies of Montana spread out forever in all directions. It was easy to see how Montana had gained its nickname of Big Sky Country.

"Your gown suits you perfectly. Was it designed for you?"

"It was my mother's."

Max shifted uncomfortably. "Ah . . . by the way . . . what is your first name."

"Deanna." She glanced at him briefly and smiled.

"This is an extremely awkward position we're in."

"I agree." *And you don't know the half of it*, she thought.

"Do I get along with my in-laws?"

How was she supposed to answer his questions when the whole situation was a deception? She decided to tell the truth when she could and change it only as much as was necessary to keep him believing that he was Kevin.

"Fine, but there's only my mother and my brother. My father left us when I was small." Deanna put down her sun visor and adjusted her sunglasses to cut down on the bright glare of the sun as it reflected off the intense whiteness of the snow.

"I'm sorry, honey." Max reached out a hand and caressed her check. It was just a gesture of compassion and caring, but it sent shock waves through Deanna.

"How *are* your in-laws?" Max quipped in an attempt to lighten the mood.

"Your mother passed away a few years back. Your father is a wonderful man. He's very worried about you and looking forward to your return home."

"Where is home?"

"Bel Air, California. It's a suburb of Los Angeles."

"Suburb as in tract homes and white picket fences?"

"Suburb as in architectural masterpieces tucked into the hills and canyons." Deanna thought about the beautiful brick-and-stone mansion she'd visited when she'd met with Alex Hilliard. The interior was decorated beautifully, fulfilling the promise of elegance made by the exterior. Max lived there, too. He also kept an apartment on the top floor of the

Hilliard Building on Wilshire Boulevard, as well as other houses and apartments scattered worldwide.

"Business must be good. Just what is it I do?"

"You're a financial investor."

Max looked at himself in the mirror on the car's sun visor. "I don't look like a financial investor."

Deanna chuckled. "What do you imagine you do look like?"

"Oh I don't know, a truck driver or a used-car salesman."

"Personally," she glanced sideways at him, "I'd have to say a professional athlete or an actor."

They drove several miles in silence.

"Where are we going?" Max asked.

"To your cabin. It's where you were staying before the accident."

"*My* cabin? Don't you mean *our* cabin?"

Deanna squelched her initial reaction to panic. "I've never been to the cabin before, so I think of it as yours."

"Now you can think of it as ours. I'm curious, though . . . why don't we just go home?"

"Your father has contacted a specialist from Boston and they're going to join us at the cabin."

"Why don't we fly to Boston and save the doctor a trip?"

"You'll have to ask them when they get here," Deanna suggested.

Max yawned. "How much farther to the cabin?"

"We'll be there in about an hour."

"Would you be offended if I took a nap?"

"Of course not. You've been through a lot. You must be exhausted."

Max stretched his legs out, leaned back, and was soon asleep. Deanna breathed a sigh of relief. She knew that there would be many more questions to come, but for now she'd gained a short reprieve. Max stirred once, when one of the bags of groceries in the trunk fell over.

Much of the fresh produce and milk that Max must have bought on his arrival had spoiled, so Deanna had stopped at the market on her way to the hospital. With the cold temperatures she hadn't had to worry about the groceries spoiling while she was at the hospital or on the drive home. In fact her biggest worry was that everything would freeze, but things had looked fine when she'd put the suitcase in the trunk. Although she would be leaving as soon as Alex and the doctor arrived, they would be staying on for at least a few days and needed to eat.

She wondered how long it took to fly from Boston to Montana. Adding another hour-and-a-half drive, she doubted that Dr. Fletcher or Alex Hilliard would be arriving until early evening. What on earth was she supposed to do with Max in the meantime?

TWO

Deanna slowly appraised the sleeping male figure by her side. She had parked the car in the garage at the cabin, but Max slept on.

His long legs were stretched at an angle across the floor space provided. His hard, muscular thighs strained against the blue denim of his jeans. The down jacket he wore concealed the upper part of what appeared to be a perfect body.

His face was softened in sleep; his thick, dark lashes lay across his cheeks. She looked downward along the strong, straight line of his nose to linger over his mouth, especially his full, sensuous bottom lip.

Deanna's heartbeat raced as she remembered the feel of his mouth moving aggressively over her own.

She reached out and ran her hand along his cheek, feeling the roughness that would become a five-o'clock shadow later in the day. In sleep, he nuzzled his face into her palm.

Deanna shivered and not entirely from the cold that was invading the car now that the heater was off. "Hey, sleepyhead, wake up."

Max's eyes flew open. He looked confused at first, then he flashed her a sexy smile, a dimple appearing in his right cheek. He sat up and looked around. "We're in a garage?"

"Yes."

"A cabin with a garage?"

Deanna smiled and nodded. Wait until he saw the four-bedroom, two-story house. Deanna had been astonished when she'd first seen it the day before. The furnishings and accessories carried an Old West theme throughout, but there was nothing primitive in the accommodations. She'd been expecting something much more rustic. To her it was a *house*, but the lack of a live-in staff ranked it as a cabin in the Hilliards' book.

They left the car, taking the envelope and Deanna's purse. It took them another two trips back to the car to retrieve the suitcase and the groceries from the trunk.

"What's for lunch? I'm starving." Max headed over to the refrigerator after all the provisions had been put away.

Deanna was puzzled by his right-at-home behavior. "Do you remember the house?"

"No, but it is ours, right?"

"Yes."

"Then this is our refrigerator?"

"Yes."

"So," he shrugged his shoulders, "let's eat."

Deanna had to laugh. He was quite a charmer, and with no apparent effort on his part.

They shared the chore of fixing lunch, keeping conversation to neutral topics. After they had eaten and returned the kitchen to order, they made their way into the living room.

"I'll start the fire," Max said as he picked up a log.

"That sounds cozy."

Max soon had the fire going in the large brick-and-stone fireplace. He joined Deanna on one of the oversized, brown leather couches.

"Shall I start another fire?" he asked as he took her into his arms.

"Max . . . please." Deanna tried to push him away.

"Max? Who in the hell is Max?" He released her.

Now she'd done it. How was she going to get herself out of this one? "It's your nickname."

He looked skeptical. "How did I ever get a nickname like Max?"

"Well . . . one of your favorite expressions is

'take it to the max'." Deanna borrowed the phrase she had seen on a T-shirt at the airport.

"I see." He gathered her to him again. "Is this strictly a business philosophy, or do I apply it to my private life as well?"

Deanna felt herself drowning in the blue-gray depths of his eyes. She was grateful when his eyelids closed over them. Her respite ended abruptly when his mouth, gently seeking, touched hers.

Deanna's lips parted in a gasp of surprise. Max took advantage of this, sliding his tongue in to explore. It swept across the front of her teeth and then moved onward to flick the sensitive roof of her mouth and stir her tongue to explorations of its own.

His hands were not idle. They moved slowly over her back and shoulders, then up to entwine themselves in her hair. One hand slipped down around her neck and slowly made its way down until it curved around the fullness of her breast, his thumb brushing across the already aroused peak.

Max pulled back a few inches. Deanna slowly opened her eyes. "Shall we 'take it to the max?' " he asked, his voice husky with desire.

Just the sound of his voice was enough to make Deanna want to say yes. Not to mention the sensations his hands and lips had sent running through her body like wildfire.

Taking her silence as an affirmative answer, Max began to unbutton her blouse. He was halfway done before Deanna snapped out of her daze.

"No. No, we can't."

"We can." He continued to undress her.

"Stop." Deanna jumped up. She rebuttoned her blouse. "Max, we—" Deanna was interrupted by the ringing of the phone. "I'll get that."

Max nodded as he leaned back into the cushions, running his hands through his hair.

"Hello?"

"Ms. Palmer, Alex Hilliard here. How's Max?"

"Fine. Would you like to speak to him?"

"In a minute. Have you happened to catch a weather report lately?"

"No, I haven't. Is something wrong?"

"A blizzard has hit the East Coast. Dr. Fletcher is stuck at the Boston airport. He'll be flying out as soon as he can, but there may be a delay of a day or two before we get to you."

"You want us to wait here?" Deanna felt the first flutters of panic starting.

"Yes, I can't take the chance of having Max seen or his condition made public. I had thought about joining you now, but Dr. Fletcher prefers to be present when I see Max for the first time."

"But . . . um . . . the name?" Deanna hoped Alex would understand that she wanted to know if she should tell Max he wasn't Kevin. She couldn't be any more specific with him right in the room.

Luckily, Alex caught her meaning. "Dr. Fletcher would like to wait on that, too."

"I see."

"I'll call again when I have more details for you."

"All right. I'll get Kevin." She held the receiver out to Max.

To give him privacy while he talked on the phone, she went out to the kitchen to make a pot of tea. She had been puzzled over what to do with Max for a few hours—now the hours had become days! It would be easier if she could tell him they weren't really married.

He was off the phone and back on the couch when she returned. His legs were stretched out in front of him as he sat watching the fire.

Deanna handed him his tea and sat down on the opposite end of the couch.

"The voice didn't sound familiar." Max sighed. "I thought I might get a mental picture of my father by talking to him." He rubbed hard against the lines furrowing his brow. "Damn, I want to remember!"

Deanna could see a mixture of anger and frustration play across his features as he searched for answers in his mind. His hands were clenched into fists. "Maybe you'll recognize him when you see him," she offered.

"When I didn't even recognize my *wife*, other than a vague feeling of having met before?"

"Well . . ." He did have a point. "You've known your father longer."

He shot her a skeptical look over the rim of his mug as he took a sip. "I don't think the amount of time you've known someone is the most important factor. I think the intensity of the relationship would have more significance." The lines in his forehead deepened. "At times I can almost feel the past. I know the memories are all in here somewhere."

"Of course they are." She couldn't even imagine how she would feel waking up in the hospital one day not knowing who she was. Then to have a stranger show up claiming they were married—would she have been as trusting as Max had been?

"Max, I'm not an expert, but I'm sure some depression is normal."

"I'm not depressed. I felt depressed at the hospital. No one knew who I was, where I'd come from. Now, I know who I am. I can't remember my past, but I have a link to it." Max set down his tea and moved closer to her. He took her mug from her hands, setting it aside also.

Deanna was expecting to be taken in his arms again, but instead he gathered her hands up into his. "There's someone special in my life, someone who belongs to me, someone who I belong to. That was the most frightening part about not remembering anything—the sheer isolation and loneliness. The feeling of not belonging anywhere."

Deanna was moved by the depth of his pain. "You belong somewhere. You're a very important person. You mean a lot to many people." She took one hand out of his and ran her fingers through his hair and along to the side of his face. She wished she could think of some way to comfort and reassure him.

"You'll remember. Dr. Sheridan said your memory loss is probably temporary. Dr. Fletcher will be here soon and he's a specialist in the field . . ." Her voice trailed off as Max stood up and walked impatiently to the fireplace.

"I'm not going to plan my future around something that might not happen. I want to build a new future."

He came back to the couch, going down on his knees before her. He laced his fingers through hers and brought her hands to his lips, kissing each gently before resting his chin on top of them. "I want us to start a whole new set of memories. Let's have a baby."

Deanna's mouth dropped open. If he'd told her that the sky was falling, she couldn't have been more surprised.

"I . . . you," she floundered. "There's something you need to know."

"One of us has a fertility problem?"

"Not that I know of, but . . ."

"Go on," he coaxed.

"We haven't been sleeping together."

Now it was Max's turn to be stunned. "We haven't been sleeping together?"

"No."

"Then it's a good thing Dr. Fletcher is coming." His eyes roved seductively over her body. "I definitely need my head examined!"

Max stood up again and started pacing back and

forth in front of the fireplace. "Was it something I did?" he asked.

"No."

"Something I said?"

She shook her head.

"You obviously still care. You came all the way up here to get me."

"K-Kevin," it was getting harder for her to call him by her ex-husband's name. "This isn't the time to go into this. Once your memory comes back, everything will fall back into place."

"Are we at least living together?"

"For the next few days, yes," Deanna hedged.

"That's not what I meant." He stood facing her, tension radiating from every muscle in his body.

Should she lie to him? She decided to tell the truth, at least to his question. "No, we don't live together." She held her breath, praying that he would drop the whole subject of their relationship.

"Are you living with anyone else?"

"No, I have my own apartment."

"Is there another man in your life?" his voice was tight and tense as though he were afraid to hear her answer.

"No, no one."

Max was quietly lost in thought. Some of the tension had left his body. He picked up the manila envelope that Deanna had set on the coffee table with her purse. He slowly went through its contents again.

Deanna waited, expecting him to denounce her as a fraud. Somehow he'd seen through her story.

"So . . ." his voice split the silence, "you don't belong to me and I don't belong to you. But you were mine once." He dropped the wedding photo into her lap. "And before we leave here, you'll be mine again."

Now what am I supposed to do? Deanna wondered as she watched Max storm up the stairs. It would have been much simpler if he had guessed the truth. She was tempted to tell him, but Dr. Fletcher felt it was best that Max not be told until he arrived and he was the expert.

She looked down at the photo in her lap. She looked so young. Had it only been four years ago? Love and hope shone from her eyes and her smile radiated happiness. Happy—yes, she'd been very happy until eighteen months after she and Kevin were married, she'd come home from work early one day to find him entertaining company—female company. They were in the shower, but the disarray of the bedding and articles of clothing scattered on the bedroom floor indicated that the festivities had started in the bedroom—their bedroom.

She'd felt betrayed, empty, and hollow—echoes of the emotions she'd felt when she'd understood for the first time that her father had left them for good and wasn't coming back. She had only been three at the time and despite Gordon telling her otherwise she was *sure* that Daddy was at work and would be coming home any time now.

After each incident she had asked herself, "What's wrong with me?" "What did I do to make Daddy leave me?" "Why did Kevin need another woman?" Hundreds of questions—questions with no answers. Questions that left her feeling flawed and inadequate.

She got up and went over to return the photo to the envelope. This was no time to indulge in a depressing introspection of her past. She had her present to think about. She could hear Max upstairs. Footsteps and water running . . . he was either getting ready to take a bath or a shower.

Taking advantage of the moment of freedom, she went to the phone to call Gordon.

"Kane Investigations, may I help you?"

"Tracy, this is Deanna. Is Gordon in?"

"Sure, one minute."

There was a brief pause before Gordon picked up the phone. "Deanna, how did it go?"

"Fine. I have him and we're at the cabin. It's going to be several days before I can come back home. The weather on the East Coast has delayed the doctor's arrival."

"Will that be a problem for you? Do you need me to come up there?"

"No, I can handle it." *You'd better start doing a better job than you have been*, she thought to herself.

"All right, but if you need anything, be sure to call."

After hanging up the phone, she walked over to the bookshelf. Choosing the latest Brandon Caruso novel, she went back to the couch and tried to read. Her mind kept going back to Max.

She had already read the first chapter of the book last night before going to bed. She had arrived at the cabin in the early evening hours. The perishable food in the refrigerator, razor and shaving cream out on the bathroom counter, and Max's wallet with his driver's license and credit cards sitting on the master-bedroom dresser let her know that if Max wasn't in the hospital, he was in the vicinity somewhere. She had slept restlessly, one ear listening for the sounds of his return. When he was still not there by morning, she hid his wallet amongst her clothes, so he would not find it and she would remember to return it to Alex Hilliard.

She thought about finding him in the hospital, his kissing her. She was still sitting there, deep in thought, half an hour later when he came back downstairs. He walked confidently, his movements just short of a strut. His muscular body was displayed to maximum advantage in the gray sweatsuit he'd changed into.

He sat down on the couch across from the one she was sitting on. He leaned back, bringing one ankle up to rest on the opposite knee. "Is that a good book?" He flashed her a heart-stopping smile.

"I haven't got very far. I just picked it out off the shelf." Half an hour ago, she added to herself.

"Listen, since you're not too involved in it yet, why don't we see if we can find a deck of cards and play a little gin rummy?"

"All right."

They soon found a deck of cards in a kitchen drawer and sat down at the table to play. Max never mentioned the discussion they'd had earlier or referred to their relationship at all. He told her stories of his friends in the hospital and asked her questions about her childhood.

"Gin." Max laid down his cards.

"Again? It's a good thing we aren't playing for money."

"Would you like to make a wager on the next hand—not for money, of course."

The fire burning in his eyes left no doubt as to what he wanted to wager and no doubt as to whom the victor would be.

He hadn't decided to let their relationship rest after all. He was up to something.

"I think it's time I started dinner. Why don't you go read."

"I'd rather help you with dinner."

Deanna would have preferred to be left alone. She was beginning to feel uncomfortable. He was charming, fun to be with, and much too sexy for her peace of mind. The oversized ego she had expected him to have was not there, but then it was probably just buried with the memories of his countless conquests.

They looked through the freezer. Besides beef and

chicken they found various cuts of elk, deer, and bear.

"Did *you* shoot this bear?" Deanna asked.

Max looked at her, one eyebrow raised.

"Oops, sorry. I forgot," she said.

"That's my line!" Max answered.

She reached up, folding her hands at the back of his neck. She smiled up at him. "You're wonderful. You've lost your memory, but you can joke about it. I wish . . ." Deanna stopped herself. She had been about to say that she wished they'd met under different circumstances.

"What do you wish for, Deanna? Ask for the moon, the world, or the stars." His eyes looked deep into hers before shifting down to look at her lips.

She yearned to forget the past and the future, to ask him for the moon, world, and stars that she had seen promised in his eyes. It took all her willpower to keep from pulling his head down where she could kiss him. "Right now I think I'd settle for closing the freezer door. I'm getting a little chilly."

Max closed the door. He moved back and looked down at where the silky material of her blouse was stretched across her breasts. "You're right." He looked up at her and grinned mischievously. "Of course it could be my nearness that initiated this response." He ran his palms up over her erect nipples.

She shuddered. "Max, we need to decide what to fix for dinner." Food was the farthest thing from her mind, but she needed to stop the heat that was spreading through her body, starting at the points where his hands continued to caress her and beginning to focus deep within her lower abdomen.

"I know what I'd like for dinner."

"Max." She reached up and moved his hands away.

"Okay," he sighed reluctantly. "Let's try the elk steaks."

They defrosted the meat in the microwave and then grilled the steaks over the built-in indoor barbecue. Deanna made a green salad and baked two potatoes in the microwave for the rest of their meal.

It was still early when they were finished eating and the clean-up of the kitchen was completed. In the living room, Max built the fire back up before joining her on the couch.

"So, I'm a financial investor?"

"Yes."

"How about you. Do you work?"

"Yes, I'm a research assistant for my brother's company."

"What kind of company is it?"

Deanna hesitated. Would he suspect something was strange if she told him the truth? "Gordon is a private investigator."

"Sounds interesting. Do you enjoy your job?"

Max continued to lull her with small talk about her work and her brother. He was easy to talk to and she soon forgot about their awkward predicament.

Deanna couldn't remember the last time she'd enjoyed an evening more.

"Do you like living alone?" Max's question immediately put Deanna back on her guard.

"It has its good points."

"What are some of the bad points of living *with* someone?"

"Anyone in particular?" Deanna teased to hide her nervousness at his new line of questioning.

"Yes, me." Max moved closer until their thighs were touching.

"Max, this is not the time to discuss our relationship. We need to get through one crisis at a time."

"The current crisis being my memory loss?"

Deanna nodded. Max took her hand, weaving his fingers through hers. "Why do I get the feeling that once this crisis is dealt with, you're going to move back into your apartment and out of my life again?"

"Max, please don't," Deanna pleaded. "It's been a long day and we're both tired. Let's go to bed and get some rest."

"I hope that's an invitation." He stood, pulling her up with him and heading for the staircase. As they passed the light switch, Deanna turned off the downstairs lights and turned on those in the upstairs hallway.

"No, it wasn't an invitation."

"Can we at least share a bed if I promise to keep my hands to myself? It's been dropping below zero at night. You might need some extra warmth."

"There's a whole closet of extra blankets. I'm sure I'll be fine." They reached the landing. "Which room would you like?"

"Yours." He pulled her close.

"No." Deanna shook her head, whether in answer to his question or as an attempt to ward off the kiss that she knew was coming.

The taste of him was becoming familiar to her—as was the burning sensation that raced through her with his every touch. As she wrapped her arms around his neck, he pulled her hips up and closer into his until she was cradled snugly against him. There was no question, he wanted her as much as she was starting to want him.

She couldn't help but wonder what it would be like to have him make love to her. He was rekindling desires within her that she had locked away years ago—desires that she didn't want rekindled.

It would be so easy to give in to him, but she knew that in the morning she would regret it.

His breathing was ragged as he pulled his mouth away from hers and buried it in the curve of her neck. "If you still plan on sleeping alone tonight, I suggest you go now."

"I didn't start this," she reminded him as she unwound her arms from around his neck and moved away from him.

"Yes, I started it, and I'm more than tempted to finish it between the sheets."

Deanna looked away from him. If he knew how

tempted she was, too, she wouldn't stand a chance. "I'll see you in the morning." She moved off toward the door of the room she'd slept in the night before.

"Sweet dreams, love," she heard him say as she closed the door.

THREE

She slept surprisingly well, considering the state of her nerves. She awoke feeling refreshed and ready to take on another day. But was she up to taking on Max? The only men in her life now were just good friends. If they tried to be anything else, they were dismissed. She'd had her share of pain and heartache; there was no way she wanted anymore.

Max wasn't so easily dismissed. They would be living together for the next few days. Since she had no choice, she chose not to worry about it. She would have to get through the day hour by hour and not worry beyond that.

She had breakfast almost ready when she heard the shower running overhead. She prepared herself mentally for Max's arrival.

He was wearing a blue knitted sweater that brought out the blue highlights in his eyes. Deanna looked down as she mumbled her good morning, but regretted it as soon as she saw the tight, faded-blue jeans he wore. He certainly filled them well—almost too well for decency.

"Breakfast smells good. I'm starving. It must be all this clean mountain air." He sat down at the kitchen table.

Deanna served the pancakes she had made and poured them each a cup of coffee. "Black?" she asked innocently.

Max set his fork down. "Surely you can remember how I take my coffee. Even if we *are* separated, we've been married almost four years." He sounded hurt, betrayed.

Four years? Where had he got that from, she puzzled. The marriage license, she remembered. "I'm sorry, I just wasn't thinking." She needed to be more careful about what she said. He would begin to think she was a complete idiot, or, even worse, he might begin to question her story.

She sat down across from him and began to eat, alternating her gaze from her plate to the view out the window. There was a large expanse of white that led to a row of snow-dusted pine trees. The darkness beyond the trees suggested that a dense forest lay beyond.

Max volunteered to clean up the kitchen, since Deanna had done the cooking. She wandered into the living room. The sound of a car engine, louder than the occasional vehicle that passed by on the main road, caught her attention. She looked out the window. Coming up the driveway was a Ford Bronco 4x4 truck. Her first thought was Alex Hilliard, but the person in the front seat was much shorter than Alex.

What if this was someone who knew Max? With a quick glance over her shoulder, she slipped out the front door, closing it noiselessly behind her.

"Good morning," the small, grandmotherly woman who climbed down from the truck greeted Deanna. "I told Ned that I saw lights over here last night. We'd begun to think that Max had gone back home without saying good-bye."

"He's been in Great Falls for a few weeks."

"I'm Alva Nelson, by the way. My husband and I live down the road. We keep an eye on the place when Max is gone. I do the cleaning inside, and Ned takes care of the yard. Since you just came up from town, I guess you don't need any groceries."

"I think we're pretty well set, thanks."

Alva's speculative gaze swept over Deanna.

Deanna realized that while Alva had identified herself, she hadn't returned the favor. "I'm Max's cousin, Deanna Palmer." *You're sinking lower and lower, DeDe. Now you're lying to sweet, helpful neighbors.*

"Are you sure you don't need anything else? I'm

on my way into town now, I have a doctor's appointment."

"No, but thank you for offering."

"If you kids are free one of these evenings, drop by. Max knows where the house is."

A pile of snow fell from a tree branch making a thumping sound. Deanna jumped nervously; she couldn't risk Alva running into Max.

Alva turned to get back into the truck. "Well, I need to be on my way. You'd better get inside. You must be cold out here without a jacket."

Deanna hadn't noticed the cold until Alva drew her attention to it. Just the fear that Max would come in search of her had kept her warm. Although she doubted that Alva knowing of Max's amnesia would do any harm, she could never be sure who knew whom and how far the information would spread.

Deanna returned Alva's wave as she went back into the house. She rubbed her hands together, trying to warm them up.

"All finished," Max called from the kitchen. "How about playing some cards?"

Deanna groaned.

"I take it you're tired of cards." He smiled at her as he came into the living room. "I've got a great idea!"

"Max . . ." she warned, correctly interpreting the gleam in his eyes.

"Hey, you can't fault a guy for trying. But seriously . . . let's explore some of the cupboards and closets and see what we can find."

Deanna consented—it sounded harmless enough. At first it felt strange going through the items stored away; but, Deanna reminded herself, this *was* Max's house. He had the right to go through any part of it that he wished to.

There were rows of cupboards underneath the bookshelves along the wall in the living room. Max started at one end and Deanna started at the other.

"I found some more cards," Max announced.

Deanna laughed. "I've got a couple of crocheted afghans, a quilt, some throw pillows . . ." Her voice faded away at the picture of Max and herself lying on the quilt in front of the fireplace, the pillows scattered around and only an afghan covering them.

"There are some definite possibilities in that list of items." Max's thoughts had obviously wandered in the same direction hers had.

"Oh look, Monopoly!" She moved on to the next cupboard in an effort to change the subject. Maybe it could erase the erotic image still imprinted in her mind.

"Remember where it is. Maybe we'll play later." Max sounded distracted.

"What have you found?" Deanna sat up on her knees and looked over the cupboard door to where Max was sitting. Her heart stopped when she saw him looking at a photo album.

Max looked up guiltily. "I'm sure these were taken before we were married."

Deanna scooted over and looked at the pictures. Many were shots of Max with male friends displaying their hunting and fishing catches. She recognized Alva in one of the pictures and assumed the man in the photo was Ned. They stood on either side of a large elk. Deanna wondered if it was the same elk they'd had part of for dinner the night before.

There was also an assortment of shots featuring women. Deanna didn't recognize any of them, but they were all attractive. Occasionally Max was in the photos with one of the women.

"I'll throw them out if they bother you," Max offered.

"Max, they're part of your past. I couldn't ask you to get rid of them." Even if she was really his wife, she wouldn't demand that he get rid of the pictures. Of course, if any of the photo subjects were to show up in the flesh, that would be a different story. "Do you recognize anyone in the pictures?"

"No, I don't." He sighed.

Deanna went back to her cupboard. With all the women Max had brought up to the cabin, she doubted that Alva had believed her when she'd claimed to be Max's cousin. "Here are some more games and a few jigsaw puzzles." What he needed games and puzzles for with all the women he'd had up here, she didn't know. *Now, now, don't get catty.*

She couldn't help wondering about the women,

though. Had he loved them or just been using them, or had they been using him? And what difference did it make to her? She'd be gone soon.

They continued their search cupboard by cupboard until they met in the middle. "Shall we do this one together?" Max asked.

"I think I can handle it." Deanna opened the door. "It looks like a stereo system of some kind." There was a radio receiver and a cassette player.

"Funny, I haven't seen any speakers anywhere." Max came up behind her. "Let's see if this works."

He leaned over her, reaching around her one side to pick out a cassette. Deanna could feel the heat radiating from his body up and down her back. As he moved closer to put the tape in the unit, he brushed up against her. The hard planes of his muscles played against her back.

"This ought to do it." He pushed the play button and Beatles music exploded around them. He adjusted the volume. "There, how's that?" His breath was warm as it moved over the side of her face.

"I wonder where the speakers are hidden," she managed to say. If he didn't move away from her soon she was going to go crazy or make a fool of herself by seducing him. Her eyes glanced over to the cupboard that held the quilt. What was it about this man that affected her this way? It had to be something beyond his good looks and terrific build. Kevin was an attractive man. He worked out on a regular basis that kept his body in great shape. Yet even the thought of making love with Kevin couldn't cause the same reaction in her body that a fully clothed Max Hilliard leaning against her back could.

Luckily, Max moved back. But he didn't move away. He only moved back far enough to allow him to turn her around to face him. "To hell with the speakers," he ground out before his mouth came down on hers.

As he kissed her, he slowly maneuvered her around until she was lying on her back. He carefully lowered himself down over her. His hands ran over her shoulders and down the length of her body. When he reached her hips, he slid his hands beneath her and lifted them up, pulling her tightly against him.

His hips and tongue took up a synchronous rhythm as he continued his assault on her senses. She clutched frantically at his shoulders trying to hold on to something solid amidst the dreamlike sensations flooding her mind and body. Deanna moaned softly against his mouth. Her tongue slid down under his, sending his thrusts across the sensitive roof of her mouth.

Max moved his lips away from hers. He placed a hot trail of kisses along the curve of her neck and over to the sensitive spot below her ear. His hands moved out from under her. They worked their way up between them and under her sweater, sliding it up and over her head. The rough texture of the carpet against her back registered only briefly as his lips found hers once more. She felt the catch of her bra loosen. Max pulled back to slide it off her. Deanna's eyes flickered open in time to see the look of hot desire and awe that flashed across his face as he looked at the sight he had unveiled. His hands trembled slightly as he reached out to touch her. Once he made contact, his caress was deliberate and skilled.

Her breasts throbbed, their peaks hardening. His mouth came down to aid his hands. Deanna closed her eyes once again, losing all sense of time. His foray may have lasted only a few minutes or it may have been hours before he raised his head.

He leaned back and pulled off his sweater and T-shirt. "It's getting hot in here."

Deanna didn't miss the double meaning in his words, but she was unable to reply as she gazed up at his bare chest. He was as perfect as she'd imagined him. His broad, muscular chest was covered by a blanket of dark hair that invited her touch. She ran her hands up over him, pleased when he shuddered in response. She moved them back down again, across the flat planes of his stomach to where his jeans rode low on his hips.

She ran her hands upward again, this time traveling up his strong arms. She stopped just short of a vividly colored bruise just below his shoulder. "Does this hurt?"

He shook his head slightly and then moved back over her, bringing their uncovered skin together, inch by slow torturous inch. When he kissed her again, her body parts lost their separate identities. All of her pulsated with the same urgent need.

Something in the back of her mind called out to her, "You can't do this." "I've got to," she answered. "You can't," the warning came again. She knew that she had to trust her instincts. Although for the life of her she couldn't remember why she shouldn't make love with Max, she knew that she had to stop.

She moved her hands away from his back and brought them between their bodies to push him away. At first he resisted her, using his greater strength and superior position to continue kissing her. But when she persisted, he backed off and let her up.

She crossed her arms over her chest. "I . . . I can't seduce you like this. It's not right."

"I thought I was doing the seducing here," his breathing was rapid, his voice husky, "and doing a damned good job of it, too!"

"You don't understand." How could she explain that she couldn't make love to him under the false pretense of being his wife.

"You're right. I *don't* understand. You want me as much as I want you." He picked up her sweater and tossed it to her.

Deanna started to shake her head.

"Don't deny it! I could feel it!" He stood up, towering over her. "Why won't you give me a chance?" When she didn't answer him, he picked up his clothes. "I'll be upstairs if you change your mind. If I stay here, I might do something one of us may regret."

Deanna watched him go. She put her bra and sweater back on. The music ended and the tape player clicked off. Deanna removed the tape, put it back in its case, and closed the cupboard.

She went into the kitchen and made herself a cup of coffee, sitting down at the table to drink it. Well, at least something good had come of her encounter with Max—she didn't have to worry about what to do for the rest of the day. As angry as he was, he probably wouldn't be speaking to her for hours. Some consolation. Her body still yearned for him, and knowing that he was just a staircase away, wanting her, too, only made it worse.

She went into the living room and sat down on the couch. She picked up the book she had abandoned yesterday but still couldn't seem to concentrate on it. Despite the coffee she had just drunk, her overwrought body had a mind of its own and she was soon fast asleep.

The sound of the phone ringing woke her up. She walked over and picked up the receiver. "Hello."

"Ms. Palmer, it's Alex Hilliard. How are things going?"

"Fine, sir. Any break in the weather back East?"

"It looks like Dr. Fletcher will be able to fly out sometime the day after tomorrow. I plan to meet him at the airport in Great Falls and we'll drive up together."

The day after tomorrow? She wanted them here now.

"Has Max shown any signs of remembering?" Alex continued.

"No. He went through a photo album and didn't recognize anyone."

Alex sighed. "It's just as well; this way Dr. Fletcher can be with him when he starts to remember."

Deanna didn't miss the confident *when* Alex Hilliard used. "Would you like to speak to your son?"

"Is he in the room with you?"

"No, he's upstairs."

"Then I'll talk to him another time. I have a call coming in on the other line. He doesn't remember me anyway."

Deanna heard the pain in Alex's voice. She wondered what had been said between them over the phone yesterday.

After she hung up the phone, she went out to the kitchen. It was late for lunch and early for dinner, but she fixed them a meal. Should she go up and get Max or should she just eat her food and let him help himself later. He was capable of heating up his own dinner and she certainly didn't feel like sitting through a meal that promised to be awkward at best.

Once the food was ready, she found that she couldn't eat without at least offering Max the chance, too. Neither of them had eaten anything since breakfast. She set the table for two and headed into the living room. Should she just holler up the stairs or go up to his room and knock? *If you stand here too long, you'll have to heat up the food again,* she reminded herself.

Finally, mustering all the courage she could find, she headed up the stairs. She wasn't even sure which room he had used. She checked the master-bedroom suite first. He was there, lying on the floor in front of the fire, an assortment of pamphlets and brochures spread out in front of him.

"Hi." Deanna walked in slowly, not sure what kind of reception to expect. "Dinner's ready, an early dinner . . . since we missed lunch . . ."

"I'll be right down." He stood up, stretching his arms high above his head without even once glancing her way.

Deanna looked away. Just the sight of him brought back the memories of the feel of him against her, the taste of his kisses, the warm smell of his skin. As he headed into the bathroom to wash up, Deanna went back downstairs.

They ate in silence. Deanna couldn't find the words to apologize for what had happened that afternoon. Max didn't seem inclined to bring it up, either. They straightened up the kitchen together.

In the living room, Max headed over to the bookcase and selected a book. "I think I'll read upstairs. Good night, Deanna."

Deanna picked up the book she had been attempting to read, turned off the lights, and went upstairs also. She had more luck with her reading this time, but had a terrible time getting to sleep.

The next morning she awakened late. When she got downstairs, Max was at the kitchen table drinking coffee.

"There are eggs and bacon on the warming tray. I thought about waking you, but you looked so peaceful, I decided against it."

Deanna filled her plate and sat across from him. She was a bit unnerved at the thought of him watching her as she slept. "I forgot to tell you. Your father called yesterday. He and Dr. Fletcher should be here some time tomorrow."

"I bet you'll be glad to see them." Max finished his coffee.

"When I'm done here, why don't we play some Monopoly?" Deanna ignored Max's remark.

"If you're sure you want to. I'm a grown man, after all. I can keep myself occupied."

"Max, I'm sorry about what happened yesterday. I never should have let things get as far as they did." She reached out and touched his arm. At first she thought he was going to pull away from her; instead he covered her hand with his free one.

"I wish you would talk to me about the past. Let me fix whatever is wrong between us. I can't fight an unknown enemy." He turned her hand over and linked it with his, palm to palm. "God, how I want you." His eyes closed as he brought her hand up to his mouth and kissed it lightly.

"Why don't we just form a truce for now?" Her voice was rough, breathless, "Please?"

His eyes blazed with his need as he opened them to look at her. "I have no choice, do I? I'll take whatever part of you you're willing to give me." He gently caressed her cheek as he got up from the table.

Deanna's stomach was full of butterflies. She couldn't eat another bite. She cleaned up her dishes and wiped off the table.

Max left the room and returned with the Monopoly game. As they played, they slowly regained the easy rapport that had existed between them until the events of yesterday had destroyed it. Deanna felt a heavy weight lift from her. She realized how much she had missed him during the afternoon and the night before.

She had to be careful; she would be leaving soon. She couldn't afford to become too attached to him. Something deep inside warned her that already it was too late. From the day Gordon had assigned the case to her, Maxwell Hilliard had been the main focus of her life. First she had been busy trying to find him, and now they were living together under the same roof.

They played for several hours. "Yesterday I found some brochures in my bedroom . . ." Max began. "There are a lot of things to see in and around Great

Falls. What do you say we drive down and check them out."

"The roads . . ." Deanna hedged. She couldn't tell him that she was afraid to take him anywhere he might be recognized.

"The roads were pretty clear when we drove up here, and it hasn't snowed since then."

"It gets dark so early. It's almost twelve already. By the time we get there it will be almost time to come back."

"We can get up early tomorrow then. We can visit the C.M. Russell Museum, the great falls of the Missouri River, check out some of the historic homes, and then pick up Dad and Dr. Fletcher at the airport. What do you think?"

"Your father said they'd drive up themselves."

"Call him and tell him the new plan."

"Let's just leave things the way they are. We can visit the sights with them."

"Maybe. Even if you don't want to go into town, we still have an afternoon to fill." Max leaned back in his chair, crossing his arms over his chest. "I think there's a ski resort nearby. I've seen cars drive by with full ski racks, and there's a jacket in the closet with a lift ticket tied on the zipper. Showdown Mountain . . . Do you want to try to find it? I'm sure one of the neighbors must know where it is."

"Why don't we play some more cards, or how about continuing with Monopoly?" Deanna was grateful that she sounded more enthusiastic than she felt about her suggestion.

"I need to get out of this house," Max said. "If you don't want to go anywhere, let's at least go out to the backyard and build a snowman."

"That sounds like fun. I'll go get my jacket." Deanna stood up.

"Don't forget your hat and gloves."

Deanna slipped on a pair of thermal underwear beneath her clothes as well as all her outer cold-weather gear. She had never played in the snow before and she thoroughly enjoyed herself.

They took a short break for lunch to eat and warm up a bit before heading back outside. They ended up building a whole snow family, complete with snow dog and snow cat. They used branches for arms, coal for facial features, and topped each with a hat.

"Shall we make them another pet or another child?" Deanna asked.

"I think it's about time we headed back inside. The sun is starting to go down."

"I didn't realize it was getting so late. I've been having so much fun . . ." she stopped as she noticed Max's expression.

"Do you realize how beautiful you are when you forget to put up any barriers between us?"

"Max . . ."

"I know, I know—our truce. Come on, let's go in." He walked over to her and put his arm around her shoulder as they headed back into the house.

They left all of their wet things in the utility room. Deanna fixed some hot apple cider and they sat down at the kitchen table to drink it.

"I didn't realize how cold I was until I started to unthaw," Max said, wrapping his hands around the mug for warmth. He looked wistfully out the window at the snow family they had built. "Did we discuss having children after we got married."

"Yes." Most married couples did, she thought to herself. She and Kevin had, but luckily they'd decided to wait.

"How many did we agree upon?"

"We hadn't settled on a specific number. We weren't in any hurry."

"But we are . . . er . . . were planning on having a family?"

"Yes." Deanna wondered how the other Maxwell Hilliard felt about children. They certainly didn't seem to suit his busy lifestyle, but the fun-loving, carefree man she'd spent the last few days with would make a wonderful father.

"We obviously weren't waiting for finances to improve before having a baby. Did we wait so that we could have more time alone together?"

"Max, please?"

He came over to where she was sitting and pulled her into his arms. Putting one hand beneath her chin, he tilted her face up. "What if I never remember, Deanna? How long are you going to make me wait before you fill me in on our past relationship?" He placed feather-light kisses on either side of her mouth. "On second thought . . . I don't want to know about the past. Forget the past with me, Deanna. Let's start over again—now. Maybe the accident was a blessing in disguise, a heaven-sent second chance for us . . ."

She put a finger on his lips to silence him. "Dr. Fletcher will be here tomorrow. Things will be settled soon." Settled? She'd be on a plane back to L.A. and Max would be going back to his life. She moved out of his arms. "I guess it's time to start dinner. Any preference?"

"Why don't you go up and take a nice hot bath followed by a nap. I'll make dinner tonight." He smiled at her, and a sharp pain ripped through her. She would miss his smiles, especially the ones like these with the mischievous glimmer in his eye.

Deanna smiled back at him. "That's an offer too good to refuse." She just hoped she wasn't slated for dessert.

FOUR

Deanna was still asleep two hours later when Max came up to escort her downstairs.

"Hey, wake up, sleepyhead." Max bounced down on the bed next to her.

Deanna opened her eyes slowly and yawned. "All that fresh air really wore me out." She sat up, stretching. Max's gaze started at her fingertips and moved down her arms. His inspection stopped when he reached her breasts, which were thrusting against her sweater. As the visual caress continued, Deanna remembered the feel of his hands and mouth on her bare skin. She could feel her nipples begin to harden. She brought her arms down and crossed them over her chest. "I'll just wash up," she muttered self-consciously. She got up quickly and went into the adjoining bathroom.

Max was still sitting on the bed waiting for her when she returned. He took her hand and led her downstairs.

The lights were off, but the fire in the fireplace and the glow of the candles on the small round table he had set up in front of it were enough. Soft classical music played in the background.

"Welcome to Chez Max." He bowed.

"I'm impressed."

"I hope the food lives up to the atmosphere." He pulled out her chair for her.

"It smells wonderful." She ran her hand over the handle of the silver knife and down the cool stem of the crystal wineglass. "Where did you find these?"

"They were tucked away on a shelf in the pantry. There's service for eight. Did we entertain up here much?" He poured the wine.

"Actually, this is my first time here."

"That's right, you mentioned that on the drive up. We'll have to make sure that it's not the last." He pushed in her chair and headed for the kitchen. "I'll be right back."

Deanna took the ivory linen napkin off her plate, slid it out of the sterling napkin ring, and placed it in her lap. Everything was so formal that she felt odd dressed in blue jeans and kelly-green pullover sweater, but Max was dressed informally also.

In the center of the table Max had made a centerpiece of pine branches and pinecones between the two silver candleholders.

"I wanted roses, but this was all I could find in the 'garden.' There's not much blooming here in October, or even alive for that matter."

"It's nice. It smells like Christmas."

Max set a salad plate in front of her. Along with lettuce, he had added a variety of fresh vegetables. He set down his own salad along with a bread basket of rolls and small bowl of butter, then with a flourish he poured wine into their glasses. He sat down across from her and placed his napkin in his lap. "I'd like to make a toast." He picked up his wineglass. "To us," he offered softly.

Deanna raised her glass to his. The clear ring of the crystal touching seemed to echo around them. As Deanna took a sip of her wine, she met Max's eyes over the rim of her glass. His eyes reflected the candle's glow.

How could she ever have thought him cold and arrogant? Because that's how those who knew him before the accident had described him! She kept forgetting that she was dealing with another Maxwell Hilliard. A Max that, so far, only she knew.

After they finished their salad, Max brought in the rest of their dinner. "Elk Bourguignon," he announced proudly. "A little help from a cookbook and a touch of imagination."

Deanna tasted it. "It's wonderful." He had also

fixed rice and broccoli. While they ate, Max kept the conversation on neutral topics, but Deanna knew there were a million questions about their relationship lurking just beneath the surface.

"Would you like dessert now or later?" Max asked when they had finished eating.

"Definitely later. I couldn't eat another bite. Everything was delicious."

"Did I cook much for you when we were living together?"

"No." She placed her napkin on the table next to her plate.

"That needs to change. You have a job, too. We should split the household chores."

"Did you, by any chance, watch *Donahue* while you were in the hospital?" she teased.

"No, I had several talks with one of the nurses. She worked a full shift and then went home and had to do all the cooking and housework. She joked about leaving her husband, but I think secretly she really wished she could leave him. If you left me because I was an inconsiderate husband, I promise I'll change."

He looked at her with his heart in his eyes. How much more of this could she stand? "Max, you have a live-in staff that handles all the household chores. You don't need to take up cooking and cleaning." Somewhere along the line, he had obviously learned to cook, though.

Max took the plates to the kitchen. Deanna followed, curious to see the condition of the kitchen. She had seen the messes her brother had created in the name of cooking. To her surprise, the only disarray were three pots on the spotless stove. He got full points for neatness as well as quality. Was there anything the man couldn't do?

"Why don't you go back and have a seat on the couch. It will just take a moment to stash the leftovers."

Deanna sat down at the end nearest the fireplace, tucking her feet up underneath her. She felt so peaceful, so at home. She could hear the wind picking up outside as a tree branch moved across a window. She knew that with the wind-chill factor added to the already frigid temperatures, it was colder than anything she'd ever experienced in her life in southern California—except maybe the freezer. Inside, with the fire going, it was comfortably warm.

She lost herself in a daydream of staying there forever. She certainly didn't miss the smog or the hustle-bustle of the city. It wasn't just the clean air and wide-open spaces that made her want to prolong their idyll. The real reason was Max. He was the added magic in the days they'd spent together.

She hadn't lived in close quarters with anyone since her divorce. She didn't feel as though she were missing anything by not having a permanent man in her life. So why was it so comforting sitting here relaxing and knowing that Max was just in the next room cleaning up. Was she finally ready to start thinking about finding someone special to share her life with again? There were several men who had been trying to get her to go out with them. Maybe once she was back home she would consider it.

Her pleasure in the idea died as she thought about the men. No, she decided, the daydream wouldn't work with anyone but Max. . . .

As if on cue, he entered the room. "Shall we play some cards?"

Deanna groaned. "I still have calluses on my fingertips from holding cards and counting Monopoly money."

"I know, but . . ." he ran his hands down his thighs, "anytime I suggest anything else, I get vetoed."

"I don't veto *all* your suggestions. Wasn't it your idea to build the snowman?"

He grunted noncommittally as he sat down next to her. He stretched his legs out in front of him and folded his hands behind his head. As he leaned back, he closed his eyes.

Deanna took the opportunity to feast her eyes on him. The flicker of the firelight accentuated his already ruggedly handsome good looks. His body, even in repose, sent out currents of sexual energy; currents that she was having trouble ignoring.

When she glanced back up to his face, she found him watching her. She felt her heartrate increase. Each breath she took became more shallow than the one before it. He didn't move closer or touch her in any way, yet the burning sensation his kisses always aroused in her was there. It started small in the pit of her stomach but soon spread throughout her body. She felt her breasts swell and her nipples harden.

She adjusted herself on the couch, thinking that it might help. It didn't. Soon the sensations were so strong that she couldn't sit still. "I . . . I'll make us some tea." She jumped up nervously. As she turned away, she saw a knowing smile light up Max's face. Somehow he knew what she was feeling and recognized her offer of tea for what it was—an evasion tactic.

Instead of turning the light on, she wandered over to the window. She pulled back the curtain and looked out. She hated the charade. She detested lying to Max about their relationship, especially when he looked at her with trust and hope of their reconciliation written all over his face. Lord, it made her feel awful.

She looked out over the snow-covered yard with its snow family. She had never seriously thought about getting remarried over the last two years since her divorce. The thought of starting over again frightened her, but as she looked at the snow couple with the children and pets she and Max had given them, she felt that somehow by staying alone she was missing out on a part of life that she wanted to experience.

Wanting children was a poor reason to get married, she knew. But she wanted more than just children; she wanted the special relationship between a man and a woman that made them mutually choose to be parents. It shocked her to realize that she could picture that with Max.

She reminded herself that the man she had left on the couch was not the same man she had researched in L.A. and that soon he would be going back to his other life and she would be going back to hers. To shut out the unexpected stab of pain this thought caused her, she turned her gaze up to the sky.

"I thought we were going to have tea?" Max entered the room.

"We are."

"Is this a secret recipe that you prepare in the dark, or would you like me to shed a little light on the subject?"

"I'll need light to make the tea, but I've been watching a cloud, or maybe it's a searchlight of some kind. It keeps appearing and disappearing."

Max joined her at the window. "Get your coat, hat, and gloves." He led her away.

"Why? What's up?"

"You'll see. Come on."

Once they were bundled up, Max led her upstairs into the master bedroom. She thought of resisting when she saw where they were headed, but he certainly wouldn't have gotten her into her cold-weather gear to seduce her. He led her across the room, through a sliding-glass door and outside onto a balcony.

Deanna was speechless. Stretched across the horizon was a glimmering waterfall whose waters flowed up instead of down.

"The aurora borealis. The northern lights," Max whispered in her ear, drawing her back against his body as he wrapped his arms around her from behind.

Deanna watched as the waterfall branched out and looked more like the flames of a fire now. A green fire that sparkled and glittered. Up above them, more to the middle of the sky, she found her "disappearing cloud" along with others that seemed to come and go as well.

"I didn't realize that the northern lights were visible this far south?"

"Yes, they're frequently seen in Montana. They're usually this light-green color here rather than the more colorful displays seen farther north."

"I wonder what causes them," Deanna pondered.

"An Eskimo legend says that they're caused by the spirits of the dead playing ball with a walrus skull. But most scientists would say that they're caused by the interaction of solar wind with the earth's magnetic field."

Deanna turned to look up at Max. "How do you know so much about them?"

"We saw them my last night at the hospital. I was curious, so I went to the hospital library the next morning and did some research."

Deanna looked to the sky once again. "It's like

looking in a kaleidoscope. . . . Max, look at the birds." Deanna pointed to a flock of migrating birds, their V-shaped formations seeming to pierce through one of the disappearing clouds even though the lights actually danced miles above.

"Flying south for the winter, no doubt. . . . Look—a shooting star." Max pointed to a brief, streaking flash of light just above the horizon.

"Yes, I saw it."

The air was cold, with just a touch of dampness. Deanna snuggled deeper into her coat and adjusted her hat even lower over her ears.

"Cold?" Max asked, drawing her closer to him.

"Yes, a little."

"Ready to go in?"

"No, not yet. I may never get to see this again. I want to remember it." She watched the horizon with its spectacular display and the sky overhead with its more subtle display. "You know, the 'disappearing clouds' remind me of the times when Gordon and I would make a tent out of a sheet. One of us would get inside and wave a flashlight around while the other watched. This looks like someone behind the sky has a big flashlight and is waving it around—only his sheet is a star-spangled black and stretches off beyond the farthest reaches of imagination."

They stood, watching. Words became unnecessary. They could feel each other's emotions: the awe, the inner peace, the feeling of smallness combined with the elation of belonging to a grander whole.

Without speaking, Max turned her in his arms and kissed her. It felt so right—a further extension of their shared experience. Her mouth opened under his, taking in his breath—so warm after the cold night air. Unlike the other kisses he'd given her, kisses from an experienced stranger, this was a kiss from someone special. He was someone she'd spent a unique evening with, someone she'd spent the last few days with and had come to care about.

Max pulled back and looked down at her. "I love you," he whispered hoarsely.

"I love you, too," Deanna answered, knowing in her heart that it was true. Somehow over the time she'd known him, he had broken down all the barriers she'd put up around her heart after her disappointing marriage to Kevin Palmer.

Max smiled. "You do?"

"Yes, I do."

He pulled her head down onto his chest, his gloved hand caressing the back of her neck beneath the collar of her jacket. "I guess wishing on a shooting star really works."

Deanna looked up at him. "In that case, I wish I'd made one."

"Start wishing, love, I promise to make them all come true."

"I wish that this moment would never end. I wish that time would stand still and we'd never have to go back to the real world."

"Something frightens you about going home, doesn't it?"

Home—if only they meant the same thing by that word. To Max it meant a place where the two of them had been and would be together. To her it was an apartment that had never seemed lonely before; but now returning to its emptiness did frighten her. The thought of living anywhere without Max's love frightened her.

"Let's not talk about it. Kiss me, Max." She pulled his head down to hers, kissing him with all the passion she had locked within her. Soon, probably tomorrow, he would no longer be a part of her life. Tonight would be her last night alone with him. This morning that thought had made her happy; now it made her sad. "Love me," she whispered.

Max groaned and pulled his mouth away from hers, to bury it in the soft curve of her neck.

Deanna took a last look at nature's "light show" as they went back into the house. Max looked from the king-size bed to Deanna and back again.

He took off his hat and gloves, putting them in his pocket before removing her hat and running his hands through her hair. "Are you sure?"

"I . . ." She was sure that it was what she wanted, but was it fair to Max? She would still be taking his love under the false pretense of being his wife; now, however, she would be giving her love to him in return. But did that make it right? Max was watching the mixed emotions playing over her face.

"I can see that you still have some reservations." He took her hand and started out of the room. "I guess knowing that you love me will have to be enough . . . for now."

He left her at the door to her room. He placed a chaste good-night kiss on her forehead and turned to go.

She opened her mouth to call him back, but then stopped herself. This was for the best, after all. She went into her room, got into her pajamas, and crawled into bed. With the new emotional upheaval in her life, she wondered if she'd be able to sleep. Surprisingly, she did.

She fell into a dream. She dreamed of Max, reliving in her dream every look, every touch, every kiss. After the final kiss on her forehead, the dream switched settings. She saw the two of them together at the Hilliard estate: in the garden, in the swimming pool, in Max's bed. There was a soft knock on the door. In her dream, Max got up to answer it.

Her conscious mind heard a door click open and a whispered, "Are you all right? I thought I heard you crying. I guess it must have been the wind. . . ."

Still on the edge of sleep, caught between her dream and reality, she felt the mattress shift with the addition of body weight.

"Max," she murmured, welcoming him back to

bed. "Who was at the door?" She reached out and placed her hand on his thigh.

He gathered her in his arms. She snuggled into the warmth of his furred chest.

His hands began roaming over her body as he placed feather-light kisses on the top of her head. He slid her onto her back, holding her in place with one hard thigh thrown across her softer one.

His lips, still touching softly, moved down across her face. He kissed up to the corner of her mouth and then slipped past it to continue on a downward course.

Deanna was still more asleep than awake. She was amazed at the increased strength of the erotic sensations her dream was arousing in her body.

She felt a light fluttering across her nipples as her silky pajama top was unbuttoned and gently pushed open. The kisses continued over the swell of her breast and around her nipple. Without being touched, it hardened, throbbing. Only after the second one was likewise coaxed did the first find relief as it was skillfully suckled—soothed by the warm moistness of his mouth and tongue. The second followed.

Deanna squirmed as the trail of kisses started moving down her body. Her pajama bottoms were lowered one step ahead.

Her body burned with passion and unfulfilled desire. She was afraid of yearning this deeply, knowing that no matter how vivid the dream became, it would only leave her frustrated and aching for Max.

"Do you want me, Deanna?" The voice was deep and husky with need. The voice alone sent sparks racing through her nerve endings.

Something wasn't right. This wonderfully sexy growl was not a figment of her imagination. Deanna's eyes flew open. "Max?" Her voice was little more than a whisper.

He moved his hard body over hers and for the first time since entering her room, kissed her lips.

It felt so good lying beneath him, his body firm, muscular, and warm. Her fingers ran through the hair on his chest and then moved up around his shoulders to pull him closer.

It took every ounce of willpower she could muster to attempt to push him away. "Max, what are you doing here? I thought . . . We can't do this."

"Do you love me?" he asked.

She hesitated briefly before she nodded. She loved him, although a month ago he probably wouldn't have given her the time of day and a month from now he might not, either, once his memory returned and he knew they had never met.

"And I love you. . . ."

Deanna looked up into his face inches above hers. She could see his features faintly in the light from the hallway. Yes, tonight the Maxwell Hilliard that was here loved her.

"Since you love me and I love you, we *can* do this. Whatever problems there are between us we'll take care of later, but I need you now."

"But . . ." Was their loving each other and needing each other enough?

"Shh . . . everything will be all right, I promise."

Deanna's last murmur of protest was lost in their kiss. Time stood still and raced by at a dizzying pace, both at the same time. Deanna's body tingled with a thousand sensations brand-new to her. She didn't remember moving her legs, but she became aware of the feel of his hair-roughened legs against the soft, sensitive skin of her inner thighs. He moved his hips back and smoothly lowered himself into her.

She was ready, aching for release. He whispered his love to her. She was unable to answer him with words, but her body showed him the love she couldn't verbalize. She felt surrounded by him; his arms curled around her, holding her close. At the same time she surrounded him, her legs wrapped tightly around him.

The darkness behind her closed eyelids began to dance with the glowing green lights of the aurora borealis. The light moved closer and closer until she became part of the energy that had lit the sky.

"Max, the lights."

"I know, love, I know."

Had she brought Max to the lights or had he brought her? Maybe this was a special magic that needed them both. Whatever—She knew she never wanted it to end.

But it did end, in an explosion of light and shudders of ecstasy that rocked through her body. Her back arched and she cried out his name. Max pushed more deeply into her and joined her in release. Together they slowly returned from the sky, leaving the lights behind, coming back to the reality of wrinkled sheets, scattered pillows, and bodies that glowed with fulfillment.

Later, Max rolled onto his back, tucking her against his side. "So, have I lost my touch?"

Deanna chuckled contentedly. "Hardly."

"Was it as good as the first time?" He lightly kissed the top of her forehead.

"The first time?" she choked.

"Yes, the first time we made love?" Max smiled down at her, a wicked gleam in his eye. "By the way, were you a virgin on your wedding night?"

Deanna swallowed. She felt uncomfortable answering questions about her wedding night, but since Max thought he had been there, it was a fair thing for him to wonder about. "Yes, I was," she answered.

"How did you get me to wait, I wonder?" His hand slid lovingly down her side, then back up to rest in the soft curve of her waist. "What was it like the first time I made love to you?"

Just thinking about it made her body tingle. "It was incredible, like nothing I'd ever felt before in my life."

Max sighed. "I wish I could remember it."

Deanna wanted to tell him that he could remember it. That it had just happened. She lay lost in thought, her fingers trailing through the crisp, dark, curling hair that fanned out across his chest.

"Was it love at first sight?" Max queried.

Deanna thought back to the moment she'd first met his eyes across the room at the hospital and remembered the tremor that had passed through her when he'd kissed her. "For me I think it was, yes. Although I didn't realize it at the time."

"What about me?"

"I don't know," she answered.

"Didn't I tell you?"

"No."

"It must have been love at first sight for me, too, because when I saw you at the hospital the other morning I felt like someone had dropped a ton of bricks on my head." His arms tightened around her and he placed several soft kisses on the top of her head.

Deanna laughed and snuggled closer to him. Never had she felt so loved, so cherished, so wanted. She refused to listen to the small voice that kept trying to remind her she was taking his love under false pretenses. He thought she was his wife. He thought he'd loved her before the accident. *You didn't earn his love; you tricked him into loving you,* the small voice insisted. *But I love him so much . . . so very much,* she repeated over and over until she had completely blocked out the small voice within.

FIVE

Deanna woke up several times during the night. Max woke also. A look, a smile—every contact between them—was enough to start them loving again. Each time was better, as they became more familiar with each other's bodies—discovering all the erotically sensitive areas.

They slept in the next morning, recuperating from their long night. Deanna woke first. She put on her robe and quietly went downstairs.

She hummed quietly to herself as she fixed breakfast. Once everything was ready, she set it on a tray and returned to the bedroom.

"You're awake already. I wanted to surprise you." She was disappointed to see Max watching her as she entered the room.

"Then you should have kept the coffee aroma downstairs in the kitchen."

Max sat up. Deanna watched the outline of his body beneath the sheet as he adjusted his position. She set the tray over his lap.

Before joining him on the bed, she walked over to the window and opened the curtain. Sometime after they'd gone to bed, leaden gray clouds had filled in the sky. Fluffy clusters of snowflakes floated slowly down from them, building up the already existing piles of snow.

"It's beautiful," Deanna said. "I've never seen snow fall before."

"Get over here and eat, then we'll go for a walk in it." Max patted the bed next to him.

Deanna curled up next to him. As they ate, she kept watching the window. "It looks just like I always imagined it would. My grandmother used to have one of those glass balls with the winter scenes inside that you could shake to make it snow inside. I used to picture what it must look like to someone who was inside the little cottage. . . ." Her voice drifted off in wonderment.

"And it looked like this?" Max asked.

"Yes." Deanna nodded. She turned to Max and smiled. "But I never imagined myself watching snow fall while having breakfast in bed with a very handsome and very undressed man," she added playfully.

Max reached behind her neck and pulled her

mouth to his for a coffee-flavored kiss. "If you want to get out into the snow, I suggest that you finish your breakfast before I decide to keep you right here for the rest of the day."

"As tempting as the offer is . . . I'll be ready to go out in fifteen minutes."

"Oh, really?" Max asked as his hand slipped inside her robe.

It was an hour later when they finally made it outside. They found a new dusting of snow on their snow family that almost hid the faces. All of the footsteps and tracks that they had made during their creating yesterday were now hidden beneath the fresh blanket of snow. Deanna wondered if the weather would prevent Alex Hilliard's arrival. Part of her wished desperately that it would. Since it was a gentle snowfall and not a snowstorm, she doubted that it would stop travel.

Their steps made a crunching sound as they set out across the backyard. Deanna held out her hand and caught a cluster of snowflakes on her glove. Against the black leather she could see the tiny crystalline patterns.

"It's hard to believe that with *all* these millions of snowflakes, there are no two the same."

"Here, check these," Max called out as he pitched a snowball at her. It hit the top of her head, burst open, and scattered snow into her face.

"I suppose you think that was funny," she replied as she bent down to return the favor.

In no time at all, the smooth expanse of snow that had been the yard was as full of craters as the moon.

"Enough!" Deanna cried, exhausted.

"Giving up already?"

"I'm not giving up, I just think it's time we went for our walk."

"You're giving up," Max laughed, sweeping her into his arms, and kissing her thoroughly before taking her by the hand.

They walked through the evergreen trees, always keeping the house within sight since Deanna was unfamiliar with the area and Max didn't remember it.

Their breath came out in white puffs, and the air they inhaled was bitterly cold. But neither of them noticed the cold. There was too much magic in the white wonderland they walked through. Fluffy piles of snow lay on top of the tree branches, while the tips of the pine needles glistened with tiny ice crystals. Deanna had never realized how many shades of white there were: the clear glittering white; the opaque white; white tinted different shades of blue, even deepening to purple, by shadows.

Max held Deanna close against his side, keeping his steps small to match hers. Despite the air temperature and the layers of clothing that separated them, Deanna could feel the heat radiating from him. She stopped, moved in front of him and into his arms.

"Hold me, Max." She needed his arms around her.

"Anytime." He pulled her as close to him as their heavy jackets allowed.

This was their world, their time. The love between them was new, as pure as untouched snow, as unique from other loves as one snowflake is from another.

"Don't ever leave me again," Max whispered against the top of her head.

Deanna pulled back and looked up into his eyes. "I can't promise that I won't leave you. There's even the chance that you may ask me to leave."

"Never," he bit out. "How can you say that?" Pain and confusion replaced the love and happiness she'd seen in his eyes only moments before.

"It's true."

"How could I send you away? I love you. I'm not whole without you." He placed a gloved hand against each side of her face. "I can't believe I ever let you out of my life before. I must have been a complete idiot! You're mine."

His kiss was fierce, desperate, as though he were trying to brand himself permanently into her heart and mind. Deanna returned it with equal desperation, hoping and praying that when his memory returned he would still feel the same.

"I love you, Max. I'll always love you," she whispered against his lips.

She didn't realize that she was crying until Max wiped away her tears. "If you're not careful, you'll end up with a pair of icicles hanging off your chin." He smiled down at her and kissed her lightly on the mouth.

They continued their walk. The shadow of the future had intruded on their happiness, but Deanna pushed it away. They had such a short time left alone, she wasn't about to waste the rest of it. It might be all she'd ever have.

"I've never been so cold." Deanna's teeth chattered as they removed their snow gear and put it in the clothes dryer.

"I know just the thing for that." Max led her upstairs and into the master bath. He filled the sunken tub with warm water and turned on the Jacuzzi.

He helped her out of her clothes and into the bubbling tub. After he joined her they had a short playful water fight and ended up making love. The turbulent water crashed against their skin, further stimulating their already aroused bodies.

After drying off, they crawled under the covers of the king-size bed. "Warm enough?" Max kissed the tip of her nose.

"Umm." As Deanna started to drift off to sleep, she marveled at the complete oneness she felt with Max—a closeness she'd never shared with anyone else.

A chill swept over her and the little voice returned,

"This can't last. You're living in a fantasy. The real world awaits."

Deanna ran her hand down the side of Max's face, rubbing her palm against the rough whiskers that were starting to show. In sleep, Max sighed and nuzzled his face into her hand, placing a kiss in its center.

Maybe she should tell him the truth about his identity before his father and Dr. Fletcher arrived. It might be best for their relationship, but how would it affect Max's amnesia? She knew so little about the condition, she was afraid to go against the doctor's request that he not be told.

"Max." Deanna propped herself up on her elbow and looked down at the man she loved. She placed a soft kiss at one corner of his mouth. "When the real world takes over your life again, don't think of me as just another conquest." She wiped a tear off her cheek. "Don't forget my feelings for you. Please . . . please, remember my love."

She wasn't sure how long she'd slept before she heard the phone ring. Moving slowly so she didn't disturb Max, she picked up the extension. "Hello."

"Deanna, this is Alex Hilliard. How is everything?"

Although there was no way Alex could see her, she felt herself blush as she adjusted the sheet over her bare breasts and glanced over at Max who was sleeping deeply. "Everything is fine. Are you at the airport?"

"Dr. Fletcher and I are at the hospital and have just finished speaking with Dr. Sheridan. We should be there in about ninety minutes."

"All right. We'll see you soon then."

As she hung up the phone, her vision blurred behind a glaze of tears. Time had just run out. She slipped out of the bed carefully, tucking the covers tightly around Max. He only stirred slightly, snuggling deeper into his pillow.

Deanna took the towels back into the bathroom, gathered up her clothes, and put Max's into the hamper. She went into her room and dressed.

She was grateful that Alex had called first rather than just arriving. It would have been very awkward if he and Dr. Fletcher had walked in on the two of them in bed together; although they, along with Gordon, were the ones who had put her in the precarious position of being alone with a man who thought she was his wife in the first place.

She wondered how soon they planned on telling him his true identity and whether Max would insist she stay and continue their relationship or insist that she leave. If Max wanted her to stay, would she? And if he didn't want her to stay . . . ? Her head was starting to throb.

She got a wet washcloth from her bathroom and lay down on her bed with it over her forehead. She must have dozed again, because it seemed like no time at all before she heard a door open and shut downstairs.

"Hello?" a voice called out.

Deanna sprang up out of bed. She wanted a chance to speak with Alex and Dr. Fletcher before Max woke up. She ran quickly down the stairs.

She stopped and tried to catch her breath. "Mr. Hilliard . . . ah . . . how was the trip?" Deanna bit her bottom lip. The experience she'd shared with Max felt wrong now that it had come face-to-face with the world beyond just as she'd feared it would. She felt as though she'd violated a trust. She had been hired to find Max, not sleep with him. Imagining that they actually had a chance together was nothing more than a daydream.

"The trip was fine."

The front door opened again and a uniformed chauffeur came in carrying two suitcases. "Shall I take these upstairs, sir?"

"Where's Max?" Alex asked Deanna.

"He's taking a nap. We went for a walk this morning and he was tired."

"Just leave the bags down here then, Roberts. You can take them up after my son awakens."

Deanna pictured Max's body sprawled across the bed, completely covered but with the outline of his muscular frame visible.

Deanna was introduced to Dr. Fletcher, a tall, thin man with graying hair. The three of them went into the living room and sat down.

"Would either of you like some tea or coffee?" Deanna asked.

"That sounds like a good idea," Alex answered.

Deanna excused herself and went out to the kitchen to fix the hot drinks. She took a tray back out to the living room with her.

Once she was seated, Alex asked, "Ms. Palmer, has there been any change in his behavior since I talked to you? Any signs of his remembering?"

"No, Mr. Hilliard."

"Dad?"

Deanna jumped. She turned to see Max at the head of the stairs, looking at Dr. Fletcher.

Alexander Hilliard rose. "No, Son, this is Dr. Fletcher. I'm your father."

Max reached the bottom of the stairs. He looked intently at Alex. "Yes, I see a resemblance. But," he turned to Deanna, "you called him Mr. Hilliard."

"That's right." Deanna looked down at her hands that were clenched tightly together in her lap.

"Why do my father and I have different last names?"

Deanna looked to Dr. Fletcher for help.

"Why don't you have a seat, Son." Alex motioned Max over to the couch.

Max sat down, but he sat on the edge.

"Your name is Maxwell Hilliard." Dr. Fletcher watched Max's face intently to see the effect of his revelation. "Does the name sound familiar?"

"No . . . no." Max shook his head. He turned to Alex. "You called Deanna, Ms. Palmer."

"Yes, that's her name."

Max looked at Deanna. She saw confusion and worry in his eyes before she looked away. "Are we married or not?"

Deanna had to clear her throat before she could speak. "Not."

"But the wedding picture, the driver's license . . ."

"Courtesy of Kane Investigations."

"The marriage license?"

"It's real."

"I see." Max's cold reply cut her off before she could explain that she was divorced.

Deanna started to speak, to correct Max's misconceptions, but then changed her mind. Maybe this was for the best. There was no future for the two of them beyond these four walls. Would she gain anything by telling him? It would be easier to walk away from him while he was angry at her.

"Now that my father and Dr. Fletcher are here, you'd better get back to your husband. I'm sure he misses you."

Deanna nodded and stood up. "If you'll excuse me, gentlemen." She passed the chauffeur on her way up the stairs. The man acknowledged her with a nod.

As Deanna packed, she began having second thoughts about her decision to let Max think she was still married. Should she try to get Max alone and explain? What if he did want to continue their relationship? He said he loved her, but was he really in love with her, or was he just in love with a woman he thought was his wife? What about all the women from Max's past waiting for him in L.A.—how could she compete with them? Maybe the best thing to do would be just to leave things the way they were, pack her bags, and go home.

She tried hard not to look at the bed, where they'd made love for the first time, as she gathered up her things. No regrets, she told herself. She had known that their time together would be short, just as she knew that she would always love him.

Fifteen minutes later Deanna went back downstairs. She set her suitcase at the foot of the stairs and walked over to the couches. The men stopped talking and rose as she neared. She held a smooth black leather wallet in her hands.

"All set?" Alex asked.

"Yes, sir." Her smile was tight and forced. She turned to Max, holding out the wallet. "This is yours."

Max flipped it open. "The *real* thing, I presume?" he indicated his driver's license.

"Yes."

He slipped the wallet into the back pocket of his blue jeans. "Let me get our jackets and I'll walk you out to your car."

While Max was out of the room, Deanna told Alex about the visit from Alva Nelson.

"I'll give her a call later this evening." He took a deep breath. "I appreciate all that you've done to help my son."

"I'm glad I was able to help."

The sound of a zipper behind her signaled Deanna that Max was back. He handed her her jacket, gloves, and hat and then picked up her suitcase and headed for the front door. Deanna exchanged goodbyes with Alex and Dr. Fletcher and then walked out the door Max held open for her.

They walked in silence to the garage. The only noise came from the snow compressing beneath their boots. Max opened the door, entered the garage, and loaded her suitcase into the backseat of the rental car.

"I'll call you in a month."

Deanna was startled. Could he still want to pursue a relationship with her even thinking she was married? She'd never imagined that he wouldn't just let her go.

"Why?" The question popped out before she had time to think.

"Why?" His voice was cold, as cold as the air that surrounded them. "Have you used any birth control in the last twenty-four hours?"

Deanna blushed. How could she have been naive enough to think that he still wanted her, and how could she have forgotten all about the possibility of pregnancy until now. "I . . . no."

"I thought not." He opened the driver's door for her. "You'll be hearing from me."

Deanna slid behind the wheel of the car. Her shoulder had grazed Max's as she moved past him, his movement away from her just short of a flinch. After closing the door, Max went around to the front of the car and unplugged the block heater.

Max left the garage, standing next to the house to wait for her to pull out. Deanna started the car and backed out of the garage. She pulled up next to the limousine Mr. Hilliard had come up in so that she wouldn't have to back down the driveway. She watched Max close the garage door and return to the house without so much as a glance in her direction.

The pain that shot through her was intense. Somehow she would survive this. After all, she'd survived her father's leaving and Kevin's betrayal—she'd get through this, too. She put the car into drive, put her foot on the accelerator, and headed down the driveway.

SIX

Back in L.A., Deanna buried herself in her work. She was usually the first one in in the morning and frequently one of the last to leave.

One evening several weeks after her return, Deanna worked late. She had heard Tracy lock up the outer doors several hours before she finally shut Charlie down for the night. When she left her office and headed out into the reception area, she was surprised to find Gordon there, comfortably lounging on one of the dark-green couches.

"Have a seat, DeDe. We need to talk."

Deanna sat down next to him. "What do you want to talk about?"

"You. Are you all right?"

"Me? I'm fine." Deanna gave Gordon a puzzled look.

"Then why have you been spending so much extra time here at work?"

"There's a lot to do, Gordon."

"Would you like me to hire you an assistant?"

"No, that's not necessary." She certainly didn't want to work close to anyone right now. She needed time to recover from her experience with Max. She needed time alone to heal.

"If your workload has grown too large for you—"

Deanna cut him off, "Gordon, the workload is fine. I just . . ." How could she explain the stretches of time when her thoughts were not on her work?

Gordon looked deep into her shadow-ringed eyes. "You seem more subdued since you came home from Montana. Did something happen up there that I should know about?"

"Gordon, I've always been subdued, as you put it. One life of the party is enough for any family."

"That doesn't answer my question. Did something happen?" He wasn't going to make this easy for her.

Deanna shifted uncomfortably in her seat. "Not really," she hedged.

"You and Max Hilliard were alone up there." Gordon watched her carefully, using his investigative skills. "Did he rape you?"

Deanna's laugh was hard and bitter. "Hardly."

"Did he seduce you?"

Deanna blushed. She and Gordon had always been close, but they'd never shared details of each other's sex lives. "Not exactly. . . ." She glanced over at her brother. "Gordon, he thought we were married. What was he supposed to do?" Deanna took in the shocked look on her brother's face. "Don't look at me like that."

"I'm sorry. You just took me by surprise. When I talked to you in Montana, you said you had everything under control. I thought . . ." He ran both hands through his hair.

"Hey, I thought you P.I.'s were experts at hiding emotion."

"We are—in the line of duty, but this is a personal matter. I feel responsible, since I sent you up there." He sat up and took Deanna's hand in his.

"Don't feel responsible. I'm a big girl and I take full responsibility for my actions."

"Would you like to talk about what happened?"

"I don't know. I still don't understand it myself. I'm not the promiscuous type, Gordon."

"I know," he assured her.

Deanna looked down. "There hadn't been anyone since Kevin." Her voice lowered. "It never even got close to that with the men I've dated."

Gordon turned her chin up until they were eye-to-eye. "I'm sure that isn't because they weren't willing. I don't think you've given any of them a chance."

"You're right." Deanna put her arms around him

and laid her head on his shoulder, unable to look at him as she continued. "I fell in love with Max, and it just happened. It felt so right at the time."

"Are you still in love with him?"

"Yes and no." She sighed. "I'm in love with the Maxwell Hilliard that I spent time with—a completely different man than he was before the accident and probably will be again once his memory is back."

"He hasn't contacted you since he got back?" Deanna felt Gordon's body tense up.

"Is he back?"

"I saw him the other evening when I took Shelly out to dinner."

"When I left Montana, he said he'd call me in about a month."

"Well, he's back now, and it doesn't sound as though he's taking your relationship as seriously as you are. I don't want to hurt you, DeDe, but he was out with another woman the other evening."

Knowing he was dating other women hurt; although she certainly had expected it, hearing about it still hit her hard. He could be with someone right now, even as she and Gordon talked. Were they at a restaurant? Was the table lit by candles? Were they gazing into each other's eyes? Were they holding hands? Was he going to kiss her good night? If yes, in or out of bed? Dozens of questions popped up to torture her.

"There's no reason why he shouldn't be out with

another woman. We didn't part on the best of terms." She explained the misunderstanding over the marriage license to Gordon.

Gordon pulled back and looked down at her, his expression full of concern. "You certainly believe in burning your bridges behind you."

"It seemed like the right thing to do at the time."

"And now?"

She sighed. "Now, I'm not sure."

As the days went by and Max's deadline of a month drew closer, Deanna found herself jumping every time the phone rang or someone knocked on her door at the office. She was sure he would contact her at work; she couldn't see him showing up at a married couple's home to demand if the wife was expecting his child.

She knew by now that she was not pregnant and had even thought about calling him and telling him so, just to ease the suspense of not knowing when he would appear.

On this Friday evening she had worked late again and then stopped by her mother's house for a visit. They hadn't seen much of each other lately with Deanna's extra devotion to her work and Mrs. Kane's job and church committee work.

She was in the process of opening her apartment door when she heard footsteps coming up the walkway. All of the horror stories of rape and violence flashed through her mind. There were plenty of single women in the complex and so far none of them had been attacked, but last week a woman a few blocks over had been assaulted.

She quickly entered her apartment, slammed the door, and locked the dead bolt. She leaned back against the door, her heart pounding, her breathing rapid. "Please God, just let him go away." Close to her head there was a knock at the door. Deanna held her breath. Should she try to get out of the apartment by the back exit and get to a neighbor's, or should she call the police and trust the locks on the door?

"Deanna, it's Maxwell Hilliard," he said before he knocked again.

Deanna looked out the peephole. Relief washed over her when she saw that it was Max at the door. And it wasn't only because he wasn't an unknown assailant that a flicker of pleasure shot through her. Just seeing him again was wonderful—despite all the apprehensions she'd had over the last month. But once she opened the door, the iciness in his eyes sent her spirits plummeting.

He looked wonderful in his formal evening wear. She had only seen him in sweatsuits, blue jeans, and, of course, nothing. The thought of the last sent the blood rushing to her cheeks.

"Ah . . . Mr. Hilliard, won't you come in?" Deanna moved back to let him enter the apartment. It surprised her that he had come here to see her thinking that she was still married. Was he planning to confront Kevin?

He came in without a word. He looked around before sitting down on the couch.

"Is Kevin asleep or did he go out for the evening, too?"

"Kevin's not here." So, he'd come to talk to Kevin. "To save you time, Mr. Hilliard, the answer to your question is no. I'm not expecting." She didn't understand the intense play of emotions that passed over Max's face as he looked at her flat stomach before it returned to its former iciness.

"I'm sure you were relieved." His voice sounded deeper. He cleared his throat, "Sit down, Deanna. We're going to wait for Kevin."

Deanna sat down in her rocking chair. She hoped the rocking would help to calm her frazzled nerves. Should she tell him about the divorce now or wait for him to tire of waiting and go? Would telling him bring him back into her life? Did she want that?

She looked around her apartment. It certainly wasn't up to the Hilliard standard of living. It was neat, clean, and tastefully decorated in shades of peach and yellow, but the total cost of it all was probably less than Max had paid for some of his paintings or object d'art individually.

"So . . . have you regained your memory?" Deanna cringed at her attempted change of topic. *Not too subtle, DeDe.*

"No, not yet. There is still some internal swelling."

"I'm sorry." She didn't know what else she could say. "Would you like some coffee?"

"No, thank you."

His voice was so cold. If there had been some warmth in his voice or any small sign of his love for her, Deanna would have been in his arms in a minute. But the man sitting across from her was an angry stranger.

The only sound was the occasional creak of the rocker. Max looked slowly around the room. Deanna was sure that he missed no detail. She wished that he'd accepted her offer of coffee; it would have given her something to do.

Max looked down at his watch. "How long do you intend to continue this charade?"

"Me? I don't understand. You're the one who came here."

"Yes. But how long are you going to pretend that Kevin Palmer might walk through the door?" He stood up and started toward her. "How long are you going to go on letting me think I slept with another man's wife?"

When Max was several steps from her, Deanna stood up. "You know about the divorce? How did you find out?"

"It wasn't hard. Why did you lie to me?" He didn't raise his voice, but Deanna could sense the anger behind his question.

"I didn't tell you that I was still married. You just assumed . . ."

"I did just assume . . . but, damn it, you should have corrected me. Letting me believe you were married was the same as a lie." He took another step forward, taking her upper arms in his hands. "Why?"

"I . . . I thought it would be best for us."

"Best for *us*? Us—you and me? What gave you the right to decide what was best for me?" Now his voice was rising.

"I . . . I . . ."

"I *needed* you, and you not only left me, but added the guilt of thinking I'd slept with another man's wife on top of it all."

Deanna put her hands on his shoulders. "Max . . ." She didn't know what to say to him. How could she explain her fears to him. She didn't even realize the extent of them herself. Her father had left them, her ex-husband had spent half of their married life in the arms of another woman. How was she supposed to feel sure enough of herself to compete with all the beautiful and interesting women for the attention of the much sought-after Maxwell Hilliard?

She looked up at him, all her love for him in her eyes. For a brief moment, the ice in his eyes melted and his love for her was there, too.

"Max, I'm so sorry. I thought I was doing the right thing." She reached her arms up around his neck. As her fingers came in contact with the hard, tense muscles of his neck, the warmth in his eyes vanished. He removed her hands and stepped back. "Max, to err is human."

"True and to forgive divine. I've been learning a lot about myself lately. I've been credited with a wide variety of abilities and talents, but no one has ever suggested that I'm divine—in the religious sense, that is."

"What can I do to make you forgive me?" the beginnings of tears started to build up in her green eyes. "I love you, Max. I want you to look at me the way you did in Montana."

"You should have stayed with me then, and I never would have stopped."

The tears were flowing freely now. "You make it sound like I deserted you. I left you with your father and a highly respected amnesia specialist."

"That took care of my medical needs. What about my emotional needs?" He began pacing, walking back and forth in front of her couch, looking everywhere but at her.

"Your father loves you deeply."

"Fine . . ." His voice rose in anger, "but the day you walked off and left me with him, I had no memory of him. He was a complete stranger to me, Deanna!"

She couldn't speak. Her throat was tight as she held back the sobs that threatened to escape. She held fast to the memory of their love. Closing her eyes, she could even sense again the feel of him within her and the soft movement of his breath across her face as he'd told her of his love.

She opened her eyes and looked at him. His expression was closed, his stance defensive. She drank in the sight of the man she loved. It hurt to have him deny the love she knew he felt.

Part of her longed to walk away from the pain, to get far away from him and never think of him or see him again. To build a new life and pretend she'd never even heard his name.

But as she thought of all the good times and the love they'd shared, she knew she wasn't ready to give up yet.

"Please try to see it from my point of view," she pleaded. "Your father hired me to find you. I felt guilty about your loving me. It felt like I was taking your love under false pretenses. You thought you were trying to win back your estranged wife, when actually we'd never met."

"The feelings were there before I was told you were my wife. They started the moment I lay eyes on you. Not merely because you're beautiful, either. It was something else, something inside you reaching out to me." The words were kind, loving, but their harsh delivery was at odds with the tender message.

"I know, I felt it, too," she said softly.

"Why didn't you tell me who I really was when we got to the cabin?"

"Dr. Fletcher wanted to be with you when you were told. He's the expert—I had to take his word on what was best for you. What complicated things even more is the fact that I fell in love with you."

"If you really loved me, then how could you walk away and leave me? Once I knew the truth about who we were, why didn't you tell me about the divorce and stay?" He raised his voice again.

Deanna looked down at his shoes. "I guess the bottom line is that I was afraid. Afraid that once you regained your memory, you wouldn't want me anymore." She looked into his eyes. "I couldn't face the possibility of you leaving me."

"So *you* left *me*? Does that make sense to you?" His face was an impassive wall of granite.

"Not now, no, but at the time . . ." There was still no empathy or understanding on his face.

"Well, you made your choice."

The shock of hearing the cold finality in his voice dried her tears. She stared at him, her eyes wide, confused. "But it was a mistake."

"It was a mistake all right, but that doesn't change anything. It's over and done with now."

Over and done with now . . . The words echoed through her mind long after the door had closed behind him.

Deanna walked slowly along the beach. The only sounds were the roar of the waves and the crunching of her sneakers in the wet sand. The fog was slowly rolling in, making the air feel close. She sat down on a rock and watched the water rolling in and out.

A flock of sea gulls, perched on the next set of rocks down the beach, also faced the sea.

Deanna lost the fight to hold back the tears that had been threatening to fall since Max had left her the night before. As a sob escaped her, the gulls took flight—all except one who remained on his rock and continued to watch the waves.

When the rain began to fall, Deanna headed back to the house. It belonged to Gordon, but he also had an apartment in the city where he stayed during the week and on the weekends if work or his social life kept him from getting away. Deanna knew he'd be in the city this weekend and had called him the night before and asked if she could spend the weekend at the beach house.

The windswept rain began to fall harder, the waves starting to crash fiercely on the beach. It felt right somehow. . . . The weather seemed to mirror the turmoil within her.

Once inside, she closed the drapes that covered the windows which made up the back wall of the house. She made herself an omelet and salad that she ate only a few bites of and curled up in front of the fireplace with a book that she didn't read beyond the title page. Her tears fell with the same torrential force as the rain that battered against the windows.

Deanna started to reach for another tissue, but stopped herself. "DeDe, this is not like you," she scolded herself. "All this self-pity is for the birds.

You can cry from now until doomsday and it won't change what happened."

Nothing could change what happened. She had made a mistake. She had apologized for her mistake, too. Max hadn't accepted her apology. So where did that leave her?

She knew that somewhere inside, he still loved her. She had seen it in his eyes for just a moment. Was he denying his love to hurt her or was he trying to protect himself from further hurt?

There had to be some way to make things right again. Hiding out at the beach, no matter how beautiful the scenery, wasn't going to get them back together. Maybe if she gave him a few days to think about what she had said to him, he would be more receptive to her apology.

Monday or Tuesday she would call him and ask to see him. If he refused, she'd just wait for him outside his office. Somehow she'd get him to listen to her.

She went upstairs to bed, determined in her resolve to win Max back.

Shortly after eleven o'clock Sunday night, Deanna set her suitcase inside her apartment. She slipped off her shoes as she shut the door behind her. In the dark room, the blinking red light on her telephone answering machine immediately caught her attention.

She walked over to the phone and pushed the playback button. "Deanna, this is your mother. If you're there, pick up the phone." There was a beep before the next message. "Deanna—Gordon. Call me when you get home." Another beep. "Deanna, this is Max Hilliard." As if she knew a dozen men named Max with voices that could melt ice. "Deanna . . . I . . ." there was a slight pause before he continued. "I'd appreciate it if you would call me when you get a chance." He left her his home phone number and his work number.

She looked at her watch. It was too late to call him back tonight. If only she'd come home earlier! She knew he was an early riser, so she would call him first thing in the morning before he left for work.

Her spirits were soaring as she unpacked her suitcase and got ready for bed. He had called *her*. She listened to the message over again, trying to determine his mood. His voice sounded warm, friendly—there wasn't any of the harsh anger from Friday night. What had he started to say before he changed his mind and just asked her to call him. Had he forgiven her? How was she ever going to make it through the rest of the night?

Knowing that Max was usually in his office by eight o'clock, Deanna called his home phone at seven.

"Mr. Hilliard is not in. Would you like to leave a message?" Deanna immediately matched the voice to Max's housekeeper, Mrs. Evans.

"I'll try to catch him at work, but in case I miss

him, tell him that Deanna Palmer returned his call. Thanks."

Of all the mornings for him to be out early. When she tried to call him at work, there was no answer. After dressing for work, she tried again. This time, she reached Max's secretary. Max wasn't in the office yet. She left another message.

She returned her mother's call. Mrs. Kane had called her Saturday night to see if she wanted to go to the movies with her. Deanna explained that she had been at Gordon's beach house.

Well, she knew Max had called sometime after six on Saturday night. After she talked to Gordon, she'd have an even better idea of when he'd called.

She decided to leave for work. If all went well, she might want to ask for the afternoon off, so the more work she could get done now the better.

"Deanna, there's a Mr. Hilliard for you on line four," Tracy's voice announced over the intercom just before ten o'clock.

Deanna's heart turned over in her chest. She sent up a fast, silent prayer, "Please, God, let him have forgiven me."

"Hello." Her voice quivered slightly as she spoke into the receiver.

"Deanna, this is Alex."

A heavy weight of disappointment settled over her. Luckily, she was able to keep her emotions out of her voice. "What can I do for you, Mr. Hilliard?"

"I'd like you to meet with Dr. Fletcher and myself. I'll send a car for you now, if that's convenient."

A cold shaft of fear cut through her heart. "Is Max all right, Mr. Hilliard?"

"He's fine. He regained his memory this morning, but . . . Listen, this would be easier for Dr. Fletcher to explain to you once you get here. My driver is leaving now. We'll see you soon."

The driver seemed to arrive in no time. Deanna remembered Roberts from the cabin in Montana. Time seemed to drag now as she sat in the back of Alex Hilliard's limousine. Deanna was oblivious to the plush accommodations as her mind and emotions ran in circles.

Max's memory was back! Why hadn't he called her himself? Why did Alex and Dr. Fletcher want to see her? An icy chill swept over her as the limo pulled up in front of a hospital.

"There must be some mistake. Alex said Max was fine," she told Roberts as she lowered the window between the back and front of her car.

"Mr. Hilliard is here for tests." He looked over his shoulder and took in her pale face. "Would you like me to come in with you?"

The strange look he gave her made Deanna recover her composure. "No thanks; really, I'm fine. Just a little surprised."

"You're sure?"

"Yes." She smiled to reassure him.

"All right. They're waiting for you in the staff lounge on the seventh floor." He got out of the car and came around to the back door to let her out.

Deanna moved away from the car quickly and stepped into the hospital lobby. If she hadn't clearly seen the hospital sign outside the building, she would have thought that she was in a hotel lobby.

As she made her way to the block of elevators, she noticed a gift shop. Several minutes later she came back out with an arrangement of autumn flowers, several magazines, and a deck of cards.

The elevator door opened as soon as she pushed the Up button. She then pushed the button for the seventh floor and the doors slid shut noiselessly and the car moved. As the floor-indicator light displayed a seven, the upward motion stopped with a slight jarring motion that sent her stomach reeling momentarily.

Deanna exited the elevator. Walking over to the nurses' station, she asked the attractive blonde where she could find the staff lounge.

"Are you Ms. Palmer?" The woman smiled.

"Yes, yes, I am."

"I'm Sarah Ryan. Dr. Fletcher told us to be watching for you. Right this way."

Once again Deanna was struck by how much like a hotel this hospital looked. If it wasn't for the white-clad doctors and nurses and the occasional medical supplies she saw in use, there was no difference.

As they passed one of the patient's room, Deanna

thought she heard a familiar laugh. A blushing nurse's aide came rushing out of the room, closing the door behind her and almost running into Deanna in her haste.

"I'm sorry, ma'am," the young woman apologized.

"Our star patient acting up again?" Nurse Ryan placed a comforting hand on the frazzled aide's shoulder.

Deanna was afraid to ask the identity of the "star patient," but she noted the room number—734. The rich male tones of laughter had sounded a lot like Max.

"Not much farther, Ms. Palmer." As the young woman left them to continue with her duties, Nurse Ryan began walking down the corridor again. She led Deanna into a bright, airy, comfortable room. As they entered, Dr. Fletcher and Alex Hilliard rose from the couch where they had been sitting.

"Nice to see you again, Ms. Palmer." Dr. Fletcher reached out to shake her hand. "Thank you for coming. Have a seat."

Before sitting down, Deanna thanked Nurse Ryan for her help.

"I believe Alex has told you that Max has regained his memory," Dr. Fletcher said.

"Yes. He also told me that Max was fine, so why is he hospitalized?" There was an edge of fear in her voice.

"I wanted to run a few tests."

"Why was I called?" Had Max asked for her? If he was all right, why hadn't he call her himself?

Dr. Fletcher pursed his lips, considering where to begin. "Occasionally when a patient recovers his past memories he loses the memories of the time he spent with amnesia. This seems to be the case with Max."

Deanna was stunned as Dr. Fletcher's words sunk in. Max had lost the memories of the time he had amnesia. This couldn't be happening. Just when there was a possibility that they might rebuild their relationship, Max didn't even know that they'd had a relationship.

Dr. Fletcher continued. "The last thing Max remembers before waking up this morning is swerving to avoid a deer that had run out in front of him. He was very surprised to find himself here in California."

"But if he doesn't remember any of his time with amnesia, what possible help can I be? We met for the first time in the hospital in Montana."

"I'd like to see if he has any recognition of you, in order to help determine if this new memory loss is as complete as it seems."

"He hadn't met you before the accident, either, had he, Doctor?" Deanna asked.

"No, the first time we met was at the cabin."

"Did he remember you?" Deanna held her breath, afraid of what the answer would be.

"Not at all."

SEVEN

Deanna accompanied Dr. Fletcher and Alex Hilliard out of the lounge and back down the hallway. Her palms were sweating as she clutched the floral arrangement, magazines, and playing cards.

It didn't surprise her that Dr. Fletcher stopped outside room 734. She had thought that the voice had been Max's and who else could rise to the rank of "star patient" while Max was in residence.

After a brief knock, the doctor pushed open the door and went in. Deanna followed slowly behind, Alex's hand resting supportively in the middle of her back. As with the rest of the hospital, the atmosphere here was like a high-class hotel. Deanna looked to the solitary bed in the room and the man occupying it.

It was the man with the cold, blue-gray eyes—the man she had searched for, the man she hadn't found. Deanna looked into the frosty eyes at close range for the first time—Maxwell Hilliard, the man in the photograph.

There was no sign of the Max she dreamed of nightly, the Max that had sent her senses reeling with his lovemaking, the man she loved.

"I told Nurse Ryan there was no need to call administration. It was all a misunderstanding." Max smiled at Deanna, but the smile touched only his mouth. His eyes swept over her, registering appreciation for what he saw but no sign of recognition.

"You're safe, Max. Deanna isn't from hospital administration," Alex chuckled.

"Floral delivery?" Max indicated the flowers Deanna held.

"These are for you," Deanna muttered as she set the flowers on his nightstand. "I brought you these also." She handed him the magazines and cards.

As he took them from her, their hands brushed briefly. A shock wave raced through her, and she pulled back abruptly. Max kept his head down, looking at his own hand. When he again glanced up at her, his eyes were questioning. Could he have felt it, too?

Deanna moved back a step until she was once again standing by Alex.

"How did you know I was interested in hunting and fishing?" Max's gaze bore into her own.

"Deanna is the one who found you in Montana, Max," Dr. Fletcher told him.

"Well, I certainly owe you a debt of gratitude. I'll buy you dinner after they let me out of this place." Although his smile widened, it still did not reach his eyes.

"That's not necessary, Mr. Hilliard. I was just doing my job." She was able to give him a small smile, hoping none of them could see that her heart was breaking.

"Oh, but I insist." He turned to Dr. Fletcher. "When am I being released?"

"If all goes well, I imagine I'll be releasing you sometime tomorrow."

"In time for a seven-o'clock dinner date?"

The doctor smiled. "I think that can be arranged."

"That's settled then." Max looked at Deanna. "I'll pick you up at seven."

"It's very kind of you to offer, but—"

"No excuses," he cut her off. "I want to hear all about how you found me."

There was a brisk knock on the door before it opened. "They're ready for you in X-ray, Mr. Hilliard," an orderly announced as he entered the room with a wheelchair. He picked up the bathrobe at the end of the bed and handed it to Max.

Max threw back the covers and slid his legs over the side of the bed. The black silk pajamas he wore had deep creases in them, as though they'd just been removed from a package. The orderly set Max's slippers in front of his feet. Grumbling, Max stepped into them and put on his robe. He walked over to the wheelchair and sat down.

"Why don't you stick around? I'll be back soon," he said to Deanna.

"No, I have to get back to work." A fact that she was very grateful for.

"Feel free to stop by later then," he added over his shoulder as the orderly started the wheelchair in motion.

"I'm going to go along and observe," Dr. Fletcher said to Alex.

"All right, I'll see you later." Once the two of them were alone in the room, Alex turned to Deanna. "Do you have time to join me for lunch before you go back to work?"

She wasn't sure if she would be able to eat, but she accepted the invitation. They went to a small Italian restaurant not far from the hospital. Since Alex had been there before, Deanna took his advice on what to order.

Once the waiter had left them Alex spoke. "Well, things will soon be back to normal."

Deanna thought she heard a touch of wistfulness in his tone. "I'm sure that makes you very happy."

"Yes, yes, of course it does."

Deanna looked down to hide the mist of tears forming in her eyes.

Alex sighed and reached out to cover her hand with his. "You're going to miss him, aren't you?"

Puzzled, she looked at Alex. How much did he know?

Alex continued. "Part of me is going to miss the man that he has been over the last month, too. Don't get me wrong. I love my son dearly. But we've never had a close, confiding relationship until after the accident. Max has always kept his feelings and emotions locked tightly inside himself. While he had amnesia, we became very close. . . . I'll miss that. It's been the first time since he graduated from high school that he's called me Dad instead of Alex."

"He was very warm and loving. His eyes smiled." Deanna found herself smiling at the memory.

The arrival of the waiter with their meal interrupted their conversation. They talked as they ate, but the conversation never moved back to Max. Deanna was grateful, for the subject was very painful.

Deanna jumped full force into her work that afternoon and all of the next day as well. She tried not to think of the evening ahead.

As she was leaving her office, she ran into Gordon in the hallway. "Going home on time tonight?" he teased.

"I figured since I'm on a set salary and don't get paid for overtime, I might as well," she threw back at him.

He laughed. "I thought I'd stop by Mom's on my way home. Would you like to join me?"

"I can't this evening."

Gordon looked at her questioningly. "Who's the lucky guy? Anyone I know?"

"Gordon Kane, what makes you think the reason I can't join you has anything to do with a male person?"

"Your flustered manner, for one." Gordon laughed as Deanna glared at him. "Come on, I wouldn't want you to be late for your date."

Deanna chose what she was going to wear for the evening carefully, telling herself that it was because she wanted to suit the elegant surroundings she would be dining in and had nothing to do with wanting to impress her date. The emerald-green of the dress matched her eyes and accentuated the red highlights of her hair. She looked down at the deep plunge of the neckline—she didn't remember it being quite so revealing.

She turned slowly around in front of the mirror, noticing the way the bottom half of her dress flowed with her body, the hem gently rocking against her calves. She had put her hair up, but decided to wear it down to cover more of her skin that was exposed by the draping back of the dress.

She remembered the saleswoman's reaction when she'd tried the dress on, "Gorgeous! You'll knock his socks off. In fact, I'll bet they reach Hawaii before coming in for a landing." Socks, sailing across the Pacific Ocean? An interesting image. But she didn't want to knock Max's socks off—or did she?

After arranging her hair, she was still debating whether too much of her was exposed and whether or not to change into something else when the doorbell rang. She glanced at the clock. Seven o'clock. Of course he was on time. Well, the dress would have to do.

She took a deep breath and let it out slowly before opening the door, a polite smile on her face. "Won't you come in," she managed to say despite the fact that the sight of him in the dark-blue suit made her heart pound.

His eyes made a thorough appraisal of her, the satisfied look on his face telling her that he liked what he saw. He walked into the apartment, looking it over as well. "Very soft and feminine. It suits you."

"Thank you. Would you like a drink, Mr. Hilliard?"

"The name's Max . . . and I think I'll take a rain check for now. I'll save it for a nightcap."

Deanna swallowed. The low sexy timbre of his voice implied that he had more than a nightcap planned for the end of this evening. "I'll get my purse then."

Deanna went into her bedroom. She picked up her evening bag and her shawl from the bed. She also put her discarded work clothes into the hamper and closed the closet door. *Why did you do that, DeDe?*

You aren't seriously considering letting him enter this room later tonight? The thought sent a cold chill racing through her veins.

She walked slowly back into the living room.

"All set?" Max asked.

"Yes."

Deanna locked the door behind them. As they started down the walkway, Max placed his hand on the small of her back. She could feel the heat of his hand through the fabric of the dress and the same tingling sensation she'd felt when their hands had touched at the hospital. He moved his hand, gently caressing her, as though he were experimenting, testing the physical reaction between them. Apparently, he was feeling something out of the ordinary as well.

When they reached the front of the apartment complex, Deanna was surprised to see a limousine pulled up by the curb. She knew Max had a Ferrari and had expected him to be driving it. It seemed to fit his smooth, playboy image. As they neared, the driver came around and opened the back door for them.

Deanna got into the car, Max sliding in next to her. Sitting in the middle of the seat across from them was a bouquet of white roses, fern and baby's breath. Max leaned over to pick up the flowers as the driver closed the door.

"For you." He handed the flowers to Deanna, once again smiling the smile that didn't reach his eyes.

"Thank you, Mr. Hilliard."

"Please, call me Max." He rested his arm across the back of the seat—not touching her, but close enough for her to feel uncomfortable.

"Thank you, Max." It was hard calling this cool stranger Max. The name belonged to the warm, caring man she was in love with. What could have happened to Max over the course of his life that changed his basic personality from warm to callous? Well, she wasn't going to worry about it. All she needed to do was get through this one evening so Max could express his gratitude and she could close the file on this part of her life.

"You're welcome."

They rode in silence. As Max's head was turned slightly away from her, Deanna took the opportunity to observe him in the dimly lit interior. His jaw was set in hard lines, the hand resting on his thigh, perfectly still. All of his movements since the return of his memory seemed so precise, almost mechanical.

She thought back to the time they had spent together. His movements had been free and spontaneous. She couldn't picture the man sitting beside her tapping his spoon on the table while he waited for his coffee to cool or fiddling with the salt shaker while she put the food on the table.

He slowly turned his head and caught her looking at him. "You're very beautiful," he said, then looked at her, his face full of male admiration for a female. But this same face had looked at her with love once, and the complete lack of that tender emotion now tore at her insides.

"Hey . . ." He ran a long, tanned finger across her cheek. "I meant it as a compliment. You look like you've just lost your best friend."

"In a way, I have," she murmured.

Luckily for Deanna, they arrived at the restaurant before Max could pursue the matter further.

The restaurant was as elegant as she'd suspected it would be when she'd tried to imagine where Maxwell Hilliard might take a date for dinner. There seemed to be more silverware on the table for two than she had in her cutlery drawer at home.

Once they had ordered and Max had selected an appropriate wine, he asked, "So, how did you manage to find me?"

Deanna explained how she had come to locate him in the hospital. She stopped the story at the hospital and forced her mind to stop there as well. There was no need for her to dwell on the time they had spent together.

"I do owe you a lot for being discreet and saving my special project. The entire program could have fallen apart."

"I'm glad everything worked out." She looked down, not wanting him to see the sadness in her eyes. Things certainly hadn't worked out for *her*.

"Once the resorts are open, feel free to use any of them, anytime, at my expense—a token of my appreciation."

"As I told you yesterday, I was just doing my job. You don't owe me anything." She picked up her water glass to take a drink, her throat suddenly dry.

"I know, but I think a job exceptionally well done should be acknowledged by a special reward of some kind."

As Deanna set her glass back on the table, Max reached out and took her hand. Deanna tried to pull away from him, to escape the unsettling sensations passing back and forth between their palms, but Max held fast to her, weaving their fingers together.

He looked deeply into her eyes. "You feel it, too, don't you?"

She couldn't answer him. His gaze dropped to her mouth. "I wonder what it will be like to kiss you?"

Deanna was grateful for the arrival of the waiter with their appetizers. As they ate, the conversation stayed on neutral topics. Deanna soon found herself relaxing and enjoying herself more as they progressed through each course of their meal. The food was not only delicious but artistically presented, also.

"So tell me, how did you end up a private investigator?"

"I'm not an investigator. I'm a research assistant."

Max looked surprised. "Mr. Kane sent a research assistant to find me?"

Ah . . . the missing ego! "Mr. Hilliard, Gordon was very conscientious when he chose me for your case. He needed someone he could trust. I've been with the agency since it opened; furthermore, I have all the qualifications to be an investigator—I simply prefer the work that I do. Besides, I think the fact that I successfully handled the task should count for more than my job title."

"You're right. . . . My apologies for questioning your qualifications." They ate in silence for a few minutes. "So how did you wind up working for Kane Investigations?"

"Gordon's my brother."

"Then why, I wonder, aren't you Deanna Kane?"

"I was for many years."

"Divorced?"

"Yes." Deanna realized that the unhappiness the topic was giving her came from the trouble the subject of her divorce had caused her and Max, rather than negative feelings about the divorce itself.

"Recently?"

"No, it was several years ago." Deanna skillfully shifted the conversation back to the subject of the resorts and then kept it on neutral topics. She didn't want to discuss her divorce, or any part of her personal life, with Maxwell Hilliard.

They were both too full for dessert, so they finished the meal with coffee. Deanna was surprised to see Max add a touch of cream to his. He had been drinking it black at the cabin.

After dinner they moved into the lounge where a band was playing soft, dreamy hits from the forties.

When they were seated, Max asked, "Would you like more coffee?"

"No thanks. One cup's my limit—any more and I'd be up all night."

Max smiled. "There's a lot to be said for staying up all night."

Deanna felt her color rise. She should have seen that coming and limited her refusal to "No, thanks."

"Would you like to dance?"

Deanna accepted to avoid the topic of conversation they'd fallen into. She questioned her choice, and her sanity, the moment Max took her into his arms.

The contact of his hand on hers and on her exposed back, and the warmth emanating from him, engulfed her in sensual memories of the two of them together as one. The music and the other couples around them faded away. In response to the increased pressure of the hand on her back, Deanna moved in a step closer to him, putting her head on his shoulder and closing her eyes.

Like a storm-ravaged ship clinging to the safety of its berth after valiantly battling to reach it, Deanna rejoiced in the secure haven of Max's arms. Her breasts were pressed tightly against the hard muscles of his chest. She moved her hand up to the back of his neck, spreading her fingers out and running them lightly through the coarse ends of his hair.

A shudder passed through Max's body. Every inch of him felt so achingly familiar. All the tension in Deanna's muscles melted away as she relaxed against him. They danced through several songs and would have continued, but the band took a break.

As the music ended, Deanna slowly opened her eyes. She moved back slightly and looked up at Max. The puzzled, bemused look in his eyes brought reality slamming into her full force. From his perspective, this was their first date, their first dance, and she was holding and caressing him with an intimacy meant for lovers.

Her eyes opened wide and she covered her mouth with her hand before she turned and walked quickly back to their table. She took several deep breaths before turning to face Max. "It's late. I think it's time to call it a night."

"Fine." Max smiled his half-smile—the one that brought out the dimple in his cheek.

"Your place or mine?" he asked as they waited for his car to arrive.

Deanna bit her bottom lip. She couldn't blame him for assuming she would be spending the night with him. Her behavior on the dance floor had been as obvious as an engraved invitation. "Listen . . . I'm afraid you've gotten the wrong idea—" She was interrupted by the arrival of the limo.

"Well?" Max prompted, once they were seated side by side.

"I'm sorry about what happened in there. It . . . I . . ."

Max moved closer to her and slid his arm along the back of the seat. Before he could move it down around her, she moved away. Max looked briefly annoyed, but then smiled another half-smile. His voice was smooth as he coaxed, "Honey, I understand all about cold feet. Just relax," he moved closer, "and trust me."

Deanna had heard the same line from many of the men she'd dated since her divorce. Any other approach from Max she might not have been able to handle, but this one . . .

She moved back again. "My feet are not cold. I just don't want to go to bed with you."

"That's not the message I was getting."

"I know." She looked down at her hands clenched tightly together. "Again, I apologize. It was just . . ." She couldn't tell him that the memory of their love and lovemaking had exploded around her when he held her close.

"Don't blame it on the wine—I've heard that one before," he drawled sarcastically.

"Not nearly as many times as I've heard, 'Relax and trust me!' " she threw back.

"Touché." Max laughed.

Deanna realized it was the first time that evening that she'd heard him laugh, and when she looked at him she saw a tiny spark of his smile reach his eyes. She couldn't help smiling back.

"So . . . what was it?"

"I guess I'm just a sucker for candlelight, soft music, and an attractive dance partner," she said nonchalantly, determined to keep the tone light.

"I've got candles and music in my bedroom. . . . Would you care to dance there?"

His eyes bore into hers, desire blazing in their depths. If he touched her, she would be lost. Somehow she had to outmanuever him. She thought about his apartment; she had gone through it looking for clues when he had disappeared. "Thank you, but no. I would like to compliment you on your stereo system. It's magnificent, although I hadn't realized you had it connected to your bedroom. Of course the free-style brass headboard on your bed and the paintings . . ."

"You've been in my bedroom?"

"In the line of duty." She lowered her voice and gave him a conspiratorial wink. "I've seen your sunken tub, too."

Max laughed again. "So you've discovered all my secret weapons, but is forewarned always forearmed?"

The driver pulled to the curb in front of her apartment. "I guess I should have Mark wait?" Max asked.

"Unless you feel like walking home, you'd better." Her smile kept her words from being rude.

Deanna retrieved her roses as the door opened. Max helped her out of the car.

"I'll be right back, Mark."

"Yes, sir."

Deanna and Max moved into the apartment complex. She had her key out of her purse before she reached the door. Max took it from her, inserted it into the lock, opened the door for her, and stepped back.

"It's certainly been an interesting evening, Deanna." Max leaned casually against the wall next to her door.

"Yes, it has. Thanks for dinner, Max, and for the roses."

"You're welcome."

"I'd better get these into water."

"Yes, you should." He didn't turn to go or move forward to kiss her.

"Well, good night."

"Good night, Deanna. Sweet dreams."

Deanna entered her apartment and closed the door. She'd made it through the evening. She should be ecstatic. She'd even managed somehow to discourage him from kissing her good night.

"Oh, bother!" She tossed her purse onto the couch with more force than usual. She kicked her shoes off and walked into the kitchen to find a vase.

"How dare he?" she asked the fragrant flowers as she arranged them. Once they were fixed, she carried them into her bedroom and placed them on her dresser.

She looked at herself in the mirror as she had mere hours before. In her eyes she could read the truth. She had wanted him to kiss her, hold her, make love to her. But it wasn't really Maxwell Hilliard she wanted, it was Max that she yearned for. The body was the same, but the personalities were so different.

"What about his heart . . . the man deep within, shouldn't that be the same?" she asked herself. "No matter, it's over and done with now."

"Over and done with now." The same words Max had used before he had walked out on her last Friday night.

EIGHT

"Deanna, there's a gentleman waiting for you in your office," Tracy, the agency's receptionist, informed her as she returned from lunch the next afternoon. The glazed, dreamy look in Tracy's eyes worried Deanna. Who could have affected the calm, level-headed Tracy this way?

She opened her office, stepped in, and closed the door behind her. At the sound of her entering, Max slowly swiveled her desk chair around to face her.

"Perhaps you would be kind enough to explain this?" He pointed to several slips of paper sitting in the middle of her deskpad.

Her deskpad—this was *her* office. What gave him the right to treat her like a delinquent student called before the principal?

Keeping a tight rein on her temper, she walked over and picked up the papers. The first one read: Monday, seven A.M., Deanna Palmer returned your call. She will try to reach you at the office. The second was on an office memo with the appropriate boxes filled to indicate that she had called his office Monday at quarter to eight to return his call. When she had finished reading, her anger had changed to nervous unease.

"What is it that you want explained? These seem self-explanatory to me."

"Why did you call me?" His voice was soft, but there was a hint of anger lying just below the surface.

"It's right here." She dropped the papers back on her desk. "I was returning your call."

Max stood up, putting both fists on her desk as he leaned across it. "Let's not play evasive games here. I'm not in the mood for Twenty Questions. I want some answers! Why did I call you?" His jaw was clenched so tightly, it was rimmed with white lines of anger.

"Calm down, Mr. Hilliard, and we'll . . . talk." She had seen him display this same frustrated anger when they were in Montana, when he had been reaching for memories that lay beyond his grasp.

Max sat back down. Deanna remained standing. She took a few steps to her right and stopped. "You realize that I can only speculate as to why you called me."

"Of course, but you'll have to agree that you are

in a much better position to come up with an accurate speculation than I am." He sighed impatiently. "Please get on with it."

"When I first heard your message on my answering machine, I assumed that you had called to apologize for the argument we'd had on Friday."

"I take it we've been seeing each other?"

"No—actually Friday was the first time I've seen you since you returned from Montana."

Max got out of the chair and stood by the window, his back turned toward her. "Maybe this would be easier to understand if you started at the beginning and explained how and why we ended up arguing?"

She didn't want to lie to him, but the pain of love lost was too new, too raw for her to talk about. So she told him what she could without giving away the emotional aspects of their previous encounter.

She picked up the threads of the story where she had left off last night during dinner. "After I found out that you were in the hospital, Gordon suggested that in order to maintain secrecy, we should have you released from the hospital under an assumed name. He could have come up with new identities for both of us, but to save time he obtained I.D. for you in my ex-husband's name. I had you released to me as Kevin Palmer."

She paced the length of her office as she mentally relived fragments of their time together.

"Go on," Max prompted.

"You were very angry when you found out that you were not who I said you were."

"Angry enough that we were arguing about it a month later?" he asked skeptically, turning away from the window to look at her.

She nodded. "That was the initial cause of the problem, yes." They had argued more about her not telling him of her divorce, but hadn't the problem been brought on by the initial deception about his identity?

Max came around to the front of her desk, leaning his hips back against it, his arms crossed over his chest as he watched her nervous pacing.

"So, you walked into the hospital and introduced yourself as my wife. I wonder how I reacted to that?" He rubbed his chin thoughtfully. "Did I take you in my arms?" He reached out and grabbed her wrist, pulling her gently forward.

Deanna's feet felt as though they were made out of lead. Max moved his long legs farther apart and slid his hands down her back until she was pressed intimately against him, her hands splayed across the hard wall of his chest. "I would imagine that a husband reunited with his wife would kiss her. Perhaps on the forehead." He demonstrated. "Or the eyes." He kissed each of her eyes closed. "But more than likely, here." His lips came down on hers, gently at first and then with increasing pressure.

She held back at first, just waiting for it to be over, but then the well-known smell, texture, and taste of him overwhelmed her and she surrendered to the kiss. Her lips parted and her tongue offered him an invitation to deepen the kiss. An invitation that he wasted no time in accepting.

Cradled against him as she was, there was no mistaking his arousal. She moaned softly as she acknowledged that she wanted him just as badly as he wanted her—maybe even more so, since she knew firsthand the magic they could create together. How could she survive without him? Only now did she realize how incomplete she had been this past month. Now she had the other half of herself. Now she was whole again.

His hands moved up underneath her sweater, trailing fire across her back, along her sides, until they surrounded her lace-covered breasts. His thumbs teased her already aroused nipples into full erectness. She was so wrapped up in feeling that she was oblivious to the motions of her own hands until they curled into the crisp hairs on Max's now-bare chest.

Max groaned as he pulled his mouth from hers and buried it in the soft curve of her neck. "Ah, yes, I must have kissed you. What man with breath in his body could have resisted?" Horrified, Deanna opened her eyes and tried to pull away from him. He straightened up and looked down at her. "And what else did we do, I wonder?"

As Max began to lower his lips to hers once again, she pulled away—this time succeeding. She turned her back on him to hide her tangled emotions. "I think you'd better go. I have work to finish up."

"So do I, but this setting is not conducive to what I have in mind." His voice was a whisper close to her ear. She hadn't heard him move, but he was standing right behind her. He gently pushed her hair aside and placed a kiss on the back of her neck, ending with a soft nibble before he pulled away. "There's more to your story than what you've told me and I intend to find out what it is." His tone of voice carried as much threat as his words.

"No!" Her reply came in a voice torn by emotion. She spun around to face him, her pain giving her courage.

She looked at him standing before her, his hair tousled, his shirt gaping open, his tie hanging down either side of his shirtfront. His stance, the turn of his head, the flicker of a smile on his mouth—all shouted confidence. Even as Deanna stood her ground, she wanted nothing more than to be back in his strong arms, losing herself again in his kiss.

"No?" He arched one brow in question. "I'll stop by your apartment about eight."

"Don't bother. There's nothing more that I can tell you."

"There's plenty you can tell me, but it will have to wait until tonight." He started for the door.

"Mr. Hilli— Max, your shirt," she reminded him.

He looked down and chuckled. "We certainly ought to be on a first-name basis at this point of things." He buttoned his buttons, tucked his shirttails back in, and went to work on his tie. His clothing back in order, he came to stand beside her, and placing one long finger beneath her chin, he tilted her face up. "Try to remember to call me Max, especially when you wake up in my bed. If you call me Mr. Hilliard then, you'll hurt my feelings." He placed a feather-light kiss on her lips and left, closing the door quietly behind him.

"You don't have any feelings!" Deanna answered bitterly, although the subject of her anger was out of hearing range.

What was she going to tell him this evening? She couldn't tell him they'd been alone in the cabin, fallen in love and made love. He'd expect her to jump right into his bed. His final remarks showed that that was where he expected her to end up anyway.

It wasn't just Max she had to fight on this issue, either—her own body wanted the same thing. It had its own memories tucked away, and while she knew the difference between Max and Maxwell Hilliard, her body treated them equally.

There was a sharp knock on her door before it opened and Gordon stepped in. "Excuse the interruption, but wasn't that Maxwell Hilliard who just left here smiling?" He looked puzzled as he noticed the distress on Deanna's face. He walked over to her and gave her a supportive, brotherly hug. "Hey, I didn't mean to be flip about it. I just assumed since Max was smiling that everything was all straightened out between the two of you."

Deanna told Gordon about Max regaining his memory, then losing the memory of the time they were together and the awkward position this put her in.

"I wish there was something I could do to help," Gordon offered.

"There isn't much anyone can do." Deanna wiped a tear off her cheek.

"Are you sure there isn't a chance for the two of you?"

"Gordon, you know Max's reputation . . ."

"Have you told him about the two of you falling in love?"

Deanna rolled her shoulders back, trying to remove some of the tension building up between her shoulder blades. "I don't see what good that would do." She sighed. "Talking about it has made me feel better, though. Thanks, Gordon."

"Anytime. Would you like me to be there this evening."

"No, I'm not sure how I'm going to handle the situation, but I know that it's something I have to handle on my own."

She was still unsure of herself when Max knocked on her door at eight o'clock that night. She had gotten used to seeing him dressed in suits since returning to L.A. and was jolted by the sight of him in tight denim jeans and a Harvard sweatshirt.

They exchanged greetings, and Max entered her apartment. "I had a call from a friend of mine this afternoon. Glen's a lawyer. He's having a casual get-together with a few friends to celebrate his winning a major case today. Why don't you change into something comfortable and come with me?"

"I . . ." She didn't want to go anywhere with him, but she didn't want to stay here and deal with the topic of the two of them in Montana, either. "I'll be right back. Would you like a drink?"

"No thanks."

"Have a seat then." Deanna went into her bedroom, changing into a pair of blue jeans and turquoise pullover.

"Ready?" Max stood up as she reentered the living room.

As ready as I'll ever be, she thought. "Yes."

After leaving the apartment, they walked through the cold evening air toward the street. Or at least it felt cold compared to this afternoon. At fifty degrees, it was twenty degrees warmer than the day she and Max had built their snow family.

"Happy thoughts?" Max asked.

"What?" Deanna was startled out of her memories.

"You were smiling." Instead of the limousine, tonight Max was driving his sports car. The low-slung red vehicle looked as sleek and powerful as its owner. Max opened the passenger door and helped her in. After he had joined her and pulled away from the curb, he continued the conversation. "What were you smiling about?"

"Well, I was just thinking how ironic it was that here fifty degrees is considered cold, while in Montana at this time of year if it reached fifty, they would consider it a heat wave."

"What did you think of Montana?"

"It . . . it's a beautiful state. Of course, I didn't see too much of it—just a bit of Great Falls, the road to the cabin and the area around it."

"The cabin? You were at the cabin?" Max glanced over at her before looking back at the road.

Deanna shifted uneasily in her seat. "Yes." She was angry at herself for letting that piece of information slip. She was going to have to be more careful in the future about what she said.

"Is that where we met Alex and Dr. Fletcher?" Max guessed.

"Yes."

"Were they there when we arrived?"

Deanna thought about stretching the truth a bit, but realized that Max could check her answer with Alex; however, she wasn't going to offer information about how long the two of them had been there before Alex and Dr. Fletcher's arrival. "No, we got there first."

"I see."

No, you don't see! she longed to throw back at

him. How could this cool, reserved man understand the love that had grown between them. She imagined that he was thinking in terms of the physical reaction between them, of the kiss they had shared that afternoon, and a sharp pain slashed through her heart.

They continued to ride in silence until Max turned the car into a long circular driveway and parked the car. Deanna jumped when the car door opened next to her. She hadn't noticed Max getting out and coming around to open it. He reached down to help her step out of the low seat. Instead of moving back as she stood up, he remained where he was, tucking his hands into the back pockets of her blue jeans and pulling her tightly against him.

He placed a trail of soft kisses along her jaw, moving from just below her ear and heading toward her lips. Deanna struggled within herself to find the strength to push him away, but instead her hands curled into his shoulders to brace herself for the total surrender she knew her body would give him.

Max pulled back, running his tongue across her bottom lip in a teasing motion. He was going in for the kill, but he was taking his sweet time about it.

Impatiently, Deanna's hand moved up around his neck intending to pull his mouth down onto hers. The surge of a car engine, the honk of a horn, and the glare of headlights broke through the aura of sensuality that surrounded them.

"Hey, Max, leaving already?" A car door slammed and footsteps headed in their direction. The newcomer was a man who Deanna estimated to be about the same age as Max, although he didn't hold his years as well as Max did. He was nice-looking, but compared to Max . . .? Was she fated to compare every man she met in the future to Max? She sincerely hoped not—it would make for a bleak future.

"No, Perry, just arriving." Max introduced Deanna to Perry, and the three of them walked up to the front door.

Max rang the doorbell. The next few hours passed in a whirl. Their host, Glen, and his wife, Kathy, were warm people and Deanna felt right at home. The small group Max had told her would be there turned out to be about thirty people. Deanna was sure that she had been introduced to just about every one of them, but couldn't remember all of their names.

Max stayed right by her side, until Glen dragged him and a few of the other men out back to see his new putting green. Max had asked if she minded and kissed her briefly before he left.

Deanna and Kathy continued their conversation. "Max is looking good," Kathy remarked. "We haven't seen much of him lately. Have you two known each other long?"

"Only about a month or so," Deanna replied, her mind searching for another subject to bring up.

She was saved the trouble when a pajama-clad toddler appeared in the doorway rubbing her eyes.

Kathy excused herself, picking up the small girl and heading down the hallway with her.

As soon as Kathy left, a tall, willowy blonde approached Deanna. Deanna had noticed the woman staring at her off and on throughout the evening.

When the woman spoke, her voice was loud and slightly slurred. Deanna guessed that she had had more than her share of the champagne that was flowing freely. "Enjoy him, honey, but do yourself a favor and don't fall in love with the bastard!"

Deanna could hear the room getting progressively quieter. She didn't have to look around her to know that she and the woman were quickly becoming the center of attention.

"He's nothing but pain and heartache. Don't just take my word for it . . ." She turned and pointed to a pretty brunette sitting close to her date on the couch. "Ask Sheila. She—"

As Sheila's date started across the room toward them, Deanna took the blonde's arm and led her in the opposite direction. "Let's go into the kitchen and I'll get you some coffee." She hoped this was the way to the kitchen. The waiters and waitresses who had been circulating with hors d'oeuvres and trays of champagne had seemed to appear from here and then disappear back this way when their trays were empty.

After getting a cup of coffee, Deanna led the woman into what appeared to be a study that they had passed on their way down the hall. There was a large, masculine-looking desk sitting in front of walls covered with books. One side of the room was arranged as a casual conversation area.

The woman sat down at one end of a plaid couch. "Here—try this," Deanna said as she handed the cup to the woman.

"Thanks." After several sips, she put the cup down on the end table. "I guess I should apologize," she said, sounding on the verge of tears. "It's just that you look like a nice person, and Max . . . Have a seat."

Deanna sat down in the chair across from the couch. "My name is Janet Franklin, by the way. Several years ago Max and I dated for a while . . . two weeks if you want to get technical. It seems impossible to believe, but in that short time, I fell in love with him."

Deanna had no trouble at all believing this. She'd fallen in love with him in less than one week herself.

Janet continued. "Max never made any promises to me, but there was something about the way he treated me, something about the way he looked at me and touched me that had me convinced that he loved me as much as I loved him."

Incredible technique and plenty of experience, Deanna thought to herself. She certainly knew how lethal Max could be.

"By the time the two weeks were over, my reputation was in shambles." A tear rolled down her cheek.

"Max indulged in locker-room gossip?" It didn't sound like Max to Deanna.

"No. I almost wish I could blame him. It was all my fault. A bunch of us girls were out to lunch. Several of them had dated Max in the past. I was so sure that we'd be making plans for a future together that I did some bragging . . . very specific bragging. God, I can't believe how naive I was."

Deanna got up and walked over to the desk and got several tissues for Janet. Sitting down on the couch next to the other woman, she placed a comforting hand on her shoulder.

"Word got back to the guys in the group and they all . . ." With Janet sobbing, neither woman heard the footsteps coming down the hallway and stopping beside the partially open door to the room they were in. "You don't know what it feels like to walk into a room and have every guy there believe that all he has to do to get you into his bed is to ask."

"You're wrong. I know exactly how it feels. After my divorce, I continued to socialize with the same group of people. All of the men who I had thought of as friends were now convinced that I would be both thrilled and eternally grateful to sleep with them. Even a casual date or a simple lift home ended up in a wrestling match."

Janet's tears had stopped and her eyes seemed clearer, more lucid. "What did you do?" Her voice had lost its slur.

"The same thing that I think you should do—I

found other friends. I still see some of the women from my married days from time to time, but I've stopped going to the mixed get-togethers."

"So how do you get dates?" Janet covered her mouth with her hand. "I'm sorry. It's none of my business. Besides, you are here with Max, so you're obviously not molding away in a closet." She picked up her abandoned coffee cup and took a drink.

Deanna chuckled. "I still go out in mixed company, just not that particular crowd. Most of those people worked with or went to school with my ex-husband. Now I've developed friendships with the people I work with and others who work in the same office building. There are more men in the world than the crowd in the living room, Janet."

"More than one fish in the sea?"

"Right."

"I guess I've got myself into a social rut. I've known Kathy since high school. When she married Glen, I met Max and the rest of the crowd and my entire social life has revolved around them."

"Then it's time you spread out a bit. You're a nice, attractive woman and you deserve a good man who will love you as much as you love him. You shouldn't have to settle for less." *You need to take your own advice, too,* she told herself.

"Thanks, I feel much better now." She set down the coffee cup.

There was a knock on the door as it swung open the rest of the way. Max stepped into the room.

"Deanna, is everything all right?" His stance looked calm and relaxed, but Deanna recognized the tightening of his jaw as a sign of his anger.

"Yes, everything is fine." She glanced over at Janet, who was looking down at her shoes.

"I guess I should go find Clay and see if he's ready to go." She looked up and smiled at Deanna. "Thanks for the coffee." She stood up and started across the room. When she got to Max she stopped. "Good-bye, Max."

Max nodded curtly and slammed the door behind her. "Damn!" He ran the fingers of one hand through his hair. "Ron told me what happened out there. I'm sorry, I shouldn't have left you alone."

"Max, I'm a responsible, grown woman, I can handle myself in awkward situations."

He took a deep breath and came to stand by the couch. "You're right. You certainly handled Janet's little tantrum well. Usually it takes two or three of us to get her into her date's car and on her way home."

"She just wanted a sympathetic ear and someone to understand what she was feeling. Isn't that what we all want?"

"I don't know, I've never thought about it." He reached his hand out to her. "Ready to go."

She put her hand in his and stood up. "Yes."

They said good-bye to Glen and Kathy. When Glen suggested that the four of them get together for dinner some evening, Max shrugged noncommittally. "We'll see."

Max was very quiet on the drive back to her apartment. She kept waiting for him to bring up the subject of the notes or her being at the cabin alone with him, but he didn't. When she invited him in for coffee, he accepted.

As she headed for the kitchen, he stopped her. "Coffee's not necessary, I just want to talk to you a minute."

Deanna sat down in her rocking chair, curling her legs up underneath her. Max sat down on the couch, leaning forward, his legs apart, hands folded, elbows resting on his knees.

"You're a very beautiful, desirable woman, and the thought of spending the rest of the night physically proving it to you has me aching."

Deanna could sympathize with him. The thought of the two of them making love started a throbbing ache deep within her lower body.

Max continued. "To be honest, that's exactly how I planned to end this evening . . . after we finished discussing the phone messages and the new information that we were alone at the cabin." He stood up and walked over to the window. "But somehow, at this late date, I seem to be developing a conscience." He turned around and looked at her, concern and uncertainty playing across his handsome features. "I heard part of your conversation with Janet. . . . You're not the kind of woman for a short-term affair and I'm not the kind of man who can give you anything else."

This caring and consideration couldn't be coming from cold, heartless Maxwell Hilliard.

He came to stand beside the rocking chair. "You need to take the advice you gave Janet. Find yourself a good man to love." He leaned over and placed a gentle kiss on her forehead. "Be happy. Have a good life."

For long minutes after the door closed softly behind him, Deanna sat staring at the empty spot on the couch where he had been sitting. Over the last few months her emotions had been tossed and turned every which way. Was this how it would end?

NINE

Over the next week Deanna felt out of focus. For the last month and a half her life had revolved around Maxwell Hilliard in some way: finding him, staying with him until the doctor arrived, waiting for him to contact her, dating him. All of a sudden Max was gone from the routine of her day, but he was still very much a part of her thoughts.

Deanna had Thanksgiving dinner at her mother's house along with her brother and an assortment of aunts, uncles, and cousins. Both Mrs. Kane and Gordon commented on her lack of appetite. She tried to pacify them by telling them that she thought she might be coming down with a cold, but Gordon looked unconvinced.

The next day was a holiday from work. Deanna

took the spare time to clean her apartment from top to bottom, hoping to clean Maxwell Hilliard out of her system as well. She tucked the eight-by-ten photo of him into her briefcase, intending to take it to work to file with the rest of the case documentation.

After she finished cleaning, she heated up some of the Thanksgiving leftovers that her mother had sent home with her for dinner and then took a long, leisurely soak in the tub before slipping into the oversize sweatsuit she liked to wear on cool fall and winter evenings.

She curled up at one end of the couch to read, but did more thinking than reading. She felt the same lonely emptiness that she'd felt the first night she had spent alone in her new apartment after she'd left Kevin.

Deanna jumped when there was a knock at the door. She looked at the clock "Ten-thirty. Who could be stopping by this late?" she asked herself. She glanced out the peephole and her heart skipped a beat. Max . . . What was he doing here?

She opened the door slowly. Yes, it was Max all right, splendidly decked out in a black tuxedo that fit him to perfection, emphasizing his broad shoulders. Deanna's fingers ached to roam over them.

He smiled. "Sorry to drop by so late." When she didn't say anything, he continued. "Is this a bad time?"

"No, come on in." Deanna moved back to let

him enter. "Can I get you a drink, or would you like some coffee?"

"Coffee sounds good, thanks."

Deanna went into the kitchen and started the coffee maker. "I've got some of my mother's homemade pumpkin pie here. Would you like some with your coffee?" she called out to him.

"If you're joining me."

As she cut the pie and poured the coffee, she noticed the slight tremor of her hands. She refused to speculate on Max's reasons for being here at this hour or where he'd been, dressed formally as he was.

When she reentered the living room, she found that Max had removed his jacket, untied his bow tie, unbuttoned the top three shirt buttons, and rolled up his sleeves. She tore her eyes away from the dark triangle of hair visible in the open V of his shirt. Unfortunately, the next thing to grab her attention were his suspenders, and she followed them across the hard planes of his chest drown to the waistband of his trousers. In her mind she imagined herself undoing the metal suspender clasps before tackling the hook and zipper.

She almost dropped the tray she was carrying as the vivid mental picture played itself out.

"Here, let me take that." Max came across the room toward her. Taking the tray, he walked back and set it on the coffee table. They both sat on the couch.

"This is delicious," Max said after taking a few bites of his pie. "Your mother made it?"

"Yes, it was her turn to have the family over for Thanksgiving. . . . Did you have a nice Thanksgiving?"

"It was all right. Alex and I ate at the house this year, something we haven't done since my mother passed away." Max set his empty plate back on the tray and picked up his coffee. He leaned back into the cushions and looked at her intently.

There was no way Deanna could finish eating with him studying her as if she were one of his financial spreadsheets. After taking her coffee off the tray and setting it on a coaster, she carried the dirty dishes out to the kitchen.

She took a few deep breaths to regain her composure while looking out the kitchen window into the darkness.

"I was wondering . . ." Max's voice broke the silence.

Deanna turned to find him in the doorway. Her kitchen had always seemed large before, but now it felt small and intimate.

Max continued. "The other night, you said we all wanted a sympathetic ear and someone to understand what we're feeling . . ."

"Yes, I said that."

"Are you only available for hysterical women or will you take on anyone?" He said it with a coolness that made it seem he wasn't overly concerned about her answer, but Deanna could sense the urgency behind his question.

"Why don't we go back into the living room and sit down?"

Max moved back, letting her pass him. When she headed for the rocking chair, he took her upper arm and led her over to the couch. They sat side by side, not quite touching.

"I don't know where to start." He ran his hands along his thighs. "Or how to start," he added softly.

"For starters, you could tell me how you came to be on my doorstep at ten-thirty dressed to kill."

"I guess that's as good a place as any." He took a deep breath. "I had a dinner date this evening with one of the secretaries from my attorney's office. I decided that if I was going to be able to keep my promise to stay away from you, I needed to get my social life back on track again." He picked up a ceramic duck that was sitting on the end table, moving his hands slowly over it.

Deanna was surprised at the strength of her reaction to the thought of his being out with another woman. Why should she be so upset? He meant nothing to her. This was not the man she had fallen in love with. But as she watched him nervously exploring the duck, his brow furrowing as he concentrated, she saw the man within the cold businessman persona. She saw "her Max."

At the sound of her short intake of breath, Max looked up. "Are you all right?"

"I'm fine," she lied.

He looked skeptical. "Maybe this isn't such a good idea." He started to stand up.

She put her hand on her arm to stop him. "No, please stay. I'm sorry, I didn't meant to interrupt. Go ahead."

"I don't think I can. This is much harder than I thought it would be. I guess you just can't teach an old dog new tricks. I have plenty of acquaintances and people to socialize with, but I've never had a friend to talk to or confide in."

"Never?" Deanna couldn't believe it. She thought of her own best friend, Joyce. Although Joyce was now married and living in Santa Barbara, Deanna knew that she was still there for her anytime, day or night, that she needed a shoulder to cry on or someone to share a happy event with.

"One of the drawbacks of having money. You can never be sure who is befriending you for what you've got rather than what you are. I got burned a few times as a child and finally learned not to trust anyone but myself. Once I got older, the stakes got higher and the game more complex." He set the duck down and turned toward her. "I've wandered a little off the track, haven't I?"

"There isn't really a set track when friends talk. It's not like a formal business report."

"It's been years since I've even thought about the concept of friendship and really talking to another person other than in a business context, until the other night when I overheard you and Janet. I didn't plan to eavesdrop, but something in the tone of your voice . . . I don't know how to explain it.'' He shrugged his shoulders. ''Things haven't been normal since I opened my eyes Monday morning and found myself in my bed in the apartment.'' He shook his head.

''You were surprised to be at the apartment?''

''Of course. I remembered flying to Montana, being at the cabin. Then I realized that I didn't remember going to bed the night before. I remembered getting in the truck and heading into town and that was it.'' He stood up and walked to the window, sticking his hands into the pockets of his trousers. ''I checked the date on my watch, which oddly enough was on the nightstand where I always leave it before going to bed, and waited for the *Twilight Zone* theme music to start or Rod Serling to walk out of my closet.''

''I guess it would be a bit of a shock.''

''I called Alex, and he and Dr. Fletcher came right over. Luckily, this all happened on one of Dr. Fletcher's visits. From what I've been told, he's been flying out here for a day every few weeks to check on my progress. They put me in the hospital for tests, and the rest you know.''

She knew the basic outline of the rest of his time, but he still hadn't explained the specific event that had sent him to her apartment so late in the evening.

Max walked back over to the couch. He stood

facing her, the coffee table between them. "I should be grateful for the return of my memory, but I find myself thinking more and more about the missing weeks. I keep wondering how I felt, what I did. . . . Even more puzzling is why after thirty-six years of being strong and efficient on my own, I find myself here telling you my problems. It doesn't make any sense to me. I hardly know you . . ."

Deanna bit her bottom lip. She was still reluctant to tell him the full extent of their relationship, but if she told him they had become close, it might help to alleviate some of the doubts he currently had. "In a way it's true that you hardly know me." She took a deep breath before continuing. "But we met and became friends, even though you don't consciously remember it."

"How close could we have become in just a few hours' time?"

"Max, the day you were released from the hospital in Montana, a snowstorm hit the East Coast. Dr. Fletcher was unable to leave Boston for several days. Because Dr. Fletcher wanted to be with you when you met Alex, your father delayed his arrival also. We spent several days alone together."

"Even several days isn't a very long time. Doesn't it take longer than that to become close friends?"

Deanna shrugged her shoulders. "Under *normal* conditions, I suppose it would." She took a deep breath. "But you thought we were married . . ."

Max looked thoughtful. "I guess that would start

us off on a different footing than if we'd been strangers." He walked around the table and sat back down on the couch. "But . . ."

"But?" Deanna prompted him.

Max looked down at the slim gold watch on his wrist. "I didn't realize it was getting so late." He stood up. "I know this is short notice, but do you have any plans for tomorrow?"

"Tomorrow or later today?" Deanna asked, after glancing at Max's watch.

"Later today."

"I don't have anything planned."

Max smiled. "Great. I'll call you around one o'clock and we'll make some plans."

Deanna walked with Max to the door. "Thanks," he said as he placed a quick kiss on her cheek.

After he left, Deanna leaned back against the door. She still didn't know exactly what had precipitated his visit, but she was glad that he had come. She put her hand up to her cheek, which still tingled where he had kissed her. Was it possible for them to just be friends?

Max called at eleven. "Let's have a picnic."

"Is it warm enough?" Deanna looked out the window.

"It's already seventy, and it's supposed to get up to seventy-eight."

"Not bad for Thanksgiving-weekend weather."

"It's criminal to waste it when the rest of the country is freezing today."

"Even Florida?"

"Well, probably not . . ." He chuckled. "So, can I pick you up in half an hour?"

"All right."

He was right on time, and the two of them set off. Deanna set her purse at her feet, along with a totebag containing her bathing suit and a change of clothes. "In case we decide to go swimming after our picnic," Max had said.

Max headed the powerful sports car toward the Wilshire district. They passed the Hilliard Building and continued on several more blocks. As they passed the L.A. County Art Museum, Max turned the corner.

"I thought we could have lunch here in the park and then if you'd like, we could wander through the art museum or the George C. Page Museum before heading back to my place for a swim."

Max carried the picnic basket and Deanna carried the blanket as they walked across the lawn.

"Which shall it be—the sloths or the bear?" Max indicated the life-size statues decorating the lawn.

"I think the sloths will do nicely."

Max set the basket down near a sloth, took the blanket from Deanna, and spread it out over the grass. Setting the basket between them on the blanket, Max opened it. "Let's see what we've got here."

There was an endless variety of salads and finger sandwiches, as well as iced tea to drink. Long before they reached the fruit, cheese, and tiny pastries, Deanna was full.

"I won't have to eat again for a week," she said.

"And here I was hoping to convince you to have dinner with me."

Deanna groaned. "I don't even want to see anything edible until tomorrow at breakfast."

"Breakfast . . . tomorrow? That can be arranged." Max leaned back on the blanket, his hands tucked behind his head, one knee raised.

Deanna looked at the teasing half-smile Max flashed at her. She longed to cross the few feet that separated them and kiss him. Instead, she adopted his light manner and returned, "Is that an invitation for breakfast . . . or an invitation to spend the night?"

Max cringed. "Ouch, you have an uncanny knack for seeing right through all my best lines."

"Sorry." She smiled and shrugged her shoulders.

"I guess we should set the ground rules for our relationship."

"Ground rules?" Deanna thumped the blanket with the palm of her hand.

"Figure of speech." He leaned forward, draping one arm across his raised knee. "I said last night that I wanted us to be friends, and I do want that very much." He reached out and took her hand. "On the other hand . . . you are a beautiful woman and we'd both know I was lying if I said I wasn't physically attracted to you. But I don't want that to get in the way of our friendship. I'll try to keep my libido in line if you promise to overlook my minor lapses. Deal?"

"Deal," she answered. He wanted to be friends, but what did *she* really want? She knew he would make a good friend, but unfortunately she knew he was a wonderful lover also. He seemed willing to overlook the physical attraction he felt for her. Could she do the same?

"Let's take a walk." Max stood up and pulled Deanna up with him. After storing the basket and the blanket back in the car, they explored Hancock Park, stopping to look at the exhibits along the way. They watched students digging through the thick, sticky tar to free the bones of animals that had been trapped thousands of years before.

In the George C. Page Museum they watched a short film showing how animals migrated to southern California to escape the Ice Age glaciers forming in Yosemite Valley. What was to become Los Angeles had been swampy grasslands at the time. Beneath the waters of the Rancho La Brea area, asphalt from an underground oil deposit bubbled just below the surface. Animals coming to drink the water would, many times, find themselves stuck. Unable to pull themselves free, they were easy prey for the saber-toothed cat and the American lion. What looked like easy prey often became a death trap as the predators frequently ended up stuck in the tar also.

After looking at reconstructed skeletal remains, Deanna and Max left the museum and walked over to what looked like a small lake bordering Wilshire Boulevard. A life-size replica of an Imperial Mammoth, tusks reaching skyward, appeared to be calling out a warning for others to avoid his fate.

"I can see how an animal might think this was just an ordinary water hole," Deanna remarked. As they watched, a bubble of tar rose up through the surface of the water, burst open, and then sunk back out of sight.

"Mmm . . . what a way to go. Would you like to browse in the art museum for a while or shall we save that for another day and go for a swim?"

As early evening approached, the temperature was dropping. "Is it warm enough to swim?"

Max draped his arm around her shoulder and started heading back to the car. "Of course. The pool's inside."

"Two pools?"

"One."

"Max, I've been to your house and I saw a pool outside."

"At the house. But at the apartment, the pool is inside."

"We're going swimming at your apartment? Alone?" Deanna had assumed that they would be swimming at the house and that Alex and Mrs. Nolan would be nearby.

Max gave her a puzzled look. "Yes, the staff has all gone away for the holiday weekend. But we're friends, right? I promised to behave myself. So, what's the problem?"

"Nothing," Deanna mumbled. What *was* the problem? They were just friends. She didn't have to worry about him making advances or seducing her. So why did she feel uneasy about the prospect of being alone with him in his swimming pool?

Her fears lay within herself and what she wanted. She admitted to herself that she wanted them to pick their relationship up from where it had been before he had lost his memory of the time they'd been together. They'd been at an awkward point, but she felt sure that they would have come through it and gotten back together.

Since he'd recovered his memory, Max's behavior had gone through several stages, changing from aggressive seducer to caring friend. She wondered if his love for her was still there inside him somewhere, directing him, even though he had no conscious memory of it? Was there some way for her to reach it?

Less than an hour later, they sat side by side in lounge chairs next to Max's pool. With three walls and a ceiling of lightly tinted glass, it was almost like being outside.

"The sky is such a pretty color of blue today." Deanna looked up.

"This is the third day in a row without the usual workday traffic. That and the slight breeze made for a nice, clear day."

A flock of birds flew by the window. "It seems strange sitting next to a swimming pool so high up in the sky."

"You'll get used to it."

"Do you swim often?"

Max turned over onto his side. Elbow bent, he propped up his head on one hand. "What does it say in your files, Madame Detective?"

Deanna tried unsuccessfully to keep her eyes and mind off the provocative sight of Max in his swimsuit. It was a real struggle to keep her mind focused enough to answer his question. "You swim or bike-ride every morning before work and occasionally after work if time permits?" *His attention to fitness certainly paid off,* she thought to herself.

"I have also been known to sneak up here on a lunch break."

"My sources missed that information."

"But you had a close enough answer. So, why did you ask how often I swam?" His gaze narrowed as he looked at her.

Deanna sighed. "There are times when I forget all about the information I gathered on you, how we met and . . ." She shifted her focus more to the vicinity of his shoulder, unable to continue looking him straight in the eye, "and everything that went before."

They sat in silence for a few minutes.

"What was I like when I had amnesia?" Max asked.

"Not at all what I expected." Lost in thought, Deanna's answer was unguarded, spontaneous.

"What were you expecting?"

She moved her eyes back to his face. It was hard to read his expression. Deanna was sure this was the same alert but shielded look he used in the boardroom. "I was expecting you to be a bit on the egotistical side . . ."

"A bit on the egotistical side? You mean a conceited, self-centered boor?"

Deanna laughed. "To be honest . . . yes."

He looked down and his voice dropped in volume, "Someone a lot like the man I've been since we met again."

Deanna shifted uncomfortably as his remark hit close to the thoughts she'd had when she'd entered his hospital room with Dr. Fletcher and Alex. She reached out and laid her hand on his arm. "Not the last twenty-four hours."

"Hey, do you think that means there's hope for me yet?" He looked up and flashed her a teasing smile.

"There's always hope." She smiled back.

"You still haven't answered my question. What was I like?"

Deanna took her hand off his arm and leaned back in her chair, trying to find words to describe the man he had been in Montana without giving away her feelings for him. "You were very open . . . kind . . . gentle . . ." *Charming . . . lethal . . . sexy,* she added to herself.

"Sounds like I was quite a guy." Max's voice was laced with sarcasm.

In a brief flash Deanna realized that both she and Max were making the same error in thinking. They were thinking of him as two different people—Max with amnesia and Max without amnesia.

"If anyone was listening to this conversation, they'd think we were talking about more than one person. Max, there's only one of you, and you are quite a guy."

"Right." Max stood up and walked over to the bar. Opening the refrigerator he asked, "Soda, iced tea, or something stronger."

"A soda will be fine."

Max added ice to two glasses and filled each. He returned to the lounge chairs and handed Deanna her drink.

"Open? Kind? Gentle? I've been called a lot of things in the past, but never open, kind, and gentle." He sat down. The muscles of his jaw were clenched tightly. "How did I handle the loss of my memory."

"You seemed to handle it very well, considering. You were frustrated at not being able to remember, but you were optimistic about the future."

"I thought we were married, right?" He turned his head sideways to look at her.

Deanna nodded.

"You'd think even an open, kind, and gentle fellow would head straight for the bedroom with you once you'd arrived at the cabin."

The ice in Deanna's drink rattled against the glass as she slowly raised it to her mouth to take a drink. She was doing fine until she started to lower her arm. Between her slight tremors and the condensation on the sides of the glass, she lost control, and ended up spilling it. The cold liquid and an ice cube ran down the front of her swimsuit.

Max quickly jumped up and handed her a towel. "Are you all right?"

"Yes, I'm fine. I don't think I got any on the lounge chair."

"Don't worry about the chair. It's washable. I'm sorry if I upset you. My remark was uncalled for."

"It's okay."

"Are you ready for another swim . . . this time in the pool?"

"That sounds nice." *Passage for two on the* Titanic *sounded better than the prospect of continuing their previous conversation!*

Deanna stood up and followed Max to the pool. Max dove into the deep end, surfacing in the middle of the pool. "Come on in, the water's fine."

Deanna walked over to the steps and entered slowly, letting her body adjust to the water gradually.

Max came to stand next to her. Drops of water beaded up on him. Deanna watched as one drop ran down his cheek, fell onto his chest, and continued to roll, weaving its way through the forest of dark hair. Her arm ached with the effort she had to exert on it to keep from tracing the same path with her fingers.

They set out swimming laps together. Max matched his pace to hers. When Deanna had to stop, Max continued for several more laps at a quicker pace.

As he set his feet down on the bottom of the pool, Deanna clapped, "Winner of the Gold Medal . . . Maxwell Hilliard."

"What a comedian." Max rolled his eyes. Humming a few bars of the theme from *Jaws*, he dove underneath the water. Deanna turned and began to swim as fast as she could, but it wasn't fast enough. She found herself being lifted out of the water. As the strong, masculine hands propelled her upward, she felt the clasp holding her single shoulder strap give way and the top of her swimsuit slip down to her waist.

Max lowered her back into the water, supporting her against his chest. "Thought you could . . ." His voice faded away, and the smile left his face.

They stood facing each other, bodies pressing together. Max's heart thundered in his chest, sending shockwaves through Deanna's bared breasts.

Max made a growling noise in the back of his throat as he slowly moved back two steps and dropped his arms to his sides. His eyes blazed over her. Deanna wanted to cover herself, but her arms refused to move.

When Max spoke, his voice was choked and hoarse. "You go on in and change. I think I'd better take a few more laps."

Deanna caught her bottom lip between her teeth. She took several steps backward before turning around, pulling the front of her suit up to the best of her ability. As she climbed the steps out of the pool, she could hear Max heading toward the opposite end of the pool.

She took her towel off the lounge chair, wrapped it around herself, and went back into the apartment. She had no trouble finding the guest room Max had let her use. Running on automatic pilot, she showered and dressed in the clothes she'd brought with her.

As she dried her hair with a blow-dryer, she could no longer hold her feelings and emotions in check. Being in Max's arms, bared to the waist, had left her painfully aroused. She wanted to make love to him, but although she believed what she had told Max—that there was only one of him and they needed to stop thinking of him as two people—part of her felt guilty about the strong physical desire she was feeling. As irrational as she knew it was, she almost felt as though she were being unfaithful.

He didn't remember that they'd been lovers. From his remark, she gathered that he strongly suspected, though. For the moment, Max saw friends and lovers as mutually exclusive. Why—and given time, could she change his mind? God, she hoped so.

Tears ran down her cheeks as she thought back over the short time the two of them had been together as lovers. She could hear his voice in her mind, telling her that he loved her.

The friendship was there and the physical reaction between them was still strong, but could it really be the same without the love?

TEN

Deanna had her emotions back in check and her makeup repaired before she heard Max walk down the hallway toward the living room.

She mentally reminded herself of the decision she'd made to stop looking back. The time they'd spent together in Montana would always have a special place in her heart, nothing would take that away from her. But she had to stop dwelling on it so much and look to the future—even if that meant she and Max would never be more than friends.

She found Max in the kitchen. His blue jeans stretched tight across his backside and his sweatshirt molded to his shoulders as he stood looking into the refrigerator. She hesitated in the doorway, still feeling awkward about the incident in the pool.

As the door swung shut behind her, Max turned around. "Hi. I was just trying to decide what to fix for dinner," he said, perfectly at ease.

"Max, I'm still full from lunch."

"Really?"

She nodded.

He held up a casserole dish. "My chef left me one of his specialties—veal with wild mushrooms. Are you sure I can't tempt you to join me?"

During the course of the meal the awkwardness fell away and they were back to the easy carefree togetherness they'd shared at the park. After dinner, they had coffee in the living room. Soft music played in the background.

"I've had a wonderful day." Max leaned back into the corner of the plush gray couch cushion.

"Me, too," Deanna agreed. She was sitting on the matching love seat near the end of the couch. "You still haven't explained what brought you to my apartment last night." She took a sip of her coffee.

"Does it matter?"

"I'm a little curious. I guess I shouldn't look a gift horse in the mouth, though." She smiled at him.

"A gift horse? I'm mortally wounded, madam." He feigned distress.

"So, are you going to tell me?"

Max looked deeply into her eyes, all signs of teasing fading away. "Why not?" He moved forward, setting his coffee cup on the table. He rubbed his hands together. "After all of your investigative work on my case, I'm sure it will come as no shock to you if I confess that I haven't been living the life of a monk."

Deanna nodded.

"It's also common knowledge that I don't spend a great deal of time with any one women in particular." Max rubbed his forehead before folding his arms across his chest. "I've enjoyed my lifestyle and have always been proud of my reputation. I can't understand . . ." He stood up and walked over to the fireplace. "Last night, as I told you, I was having dinner with a woman. Things were going well. She was sending all the right signals to indicate that the evening would end right where I wanted it to."

"Meaning, in your bed?" Deanna's question was almost a whisper.

"Or hers, I didn't care which." His back was still to her as he stared up at the painting above the mantel. "Once we were in the car and on the way home, instead of the usual thrill of conquest . . . all I felt was emptiness. The reputation that I'd been so proud of seemed shallow and unfulfilling."

Max turned around and looked at Deanna. His eyes burned deep into her soul.

"W-where do I fit into this?" she asked.

"After I dropped my date off, I drove around for a while, thinking. I ended up on your street. Even then I wasn't going to go to your door, but something drew me there. At first I thought . . . Damn," he swore as he drug his hands through his hair. "I can't tell you this."

Deanna stood up, set her coffee on the table next to his, and walked over to stand beside him. "Why?"

"Because then you'll realize what a self-centered egotist I really am."

"I'll admit you act like a self-centered egotist at times, but I don't think that's how you really are."

Max's mouth twisted in a cynical smile. "You don't? Would you change your mind if I told you that the reason I came to your apartment last night was to work you out of my system."

"Work me out of your system?" Did he mean what she suspected he might?

"Yes, take you to bed and break the spell you seem to have over me."

"But you didn't. . . . And in the pool . . ." Last night and today, he'd said that he wanted to be friends. Now he was telling her that he'd gone to her apartment to make love to her. Deanna was confused.

"Once I saw you, the conversation I'd overheard between you and Janet kept running through my mind. She'd said that you didn't know what it felt like to walk into a room and have every guy there believe that all he had to do to get you into his bed was to ask. You told her that she was wrong, that you *did* know how it felt." He leaned against the mantel. "My first reaction had been to think the other guys were a bunch of fools, but then it occurred to me that I was acting the same way. I thought all I had to do was ask." He shrugged his shoulders. "Then I thought about what you'd said to me about needing someone to listen. I . . . God, don't look at me like that." Max closed his eyes.

"Like what?"

Max reopened his eyes and looked down at her. "Don't look at me like you trust me, like you think I'm a *nice* guy. I'm one of those guys your mother warned you about—a rake . . . a rat . . ."

"You don't look anything like a gardening tool or a rodent, Maxwell Hilliard. It doesn't matter why you came to my apartment in the first place. The important thing is that you changed your mind."

"Even if I don't understand why I changed my mind? Why all of a sudden last night, just being with you, talking to you became more important than seducing you."

"Doesn't that prove to you that you're not the rake or rat that you think you are?"

Max's gaze moved from her eyes down to her mouth and then down to the neckline of her sweater. "No? Right now I'm having serious regrets about not making love to you in the pool. I had you half naked in my arms; I could feel you tremble against me. I sent you away, and I've been calling myself a fool ever since."

"But you *did* stop. You *did* send me away. Doesn't that mean anything to you?"

"If I'd asked for permission to continue, would you have said no?"

Deanna's chest felt tight as she struggled to breathe normally. "No." She started to reach her hand out to touch his arm.

Max took a step backward. "Don't. I'm sure I don't have the strength to stop a second time. Despite my beginning intentions, I hope we can still be friends."

Deanna wanted to ask him why they would need to stop, why they couldn't be friends and lovers, but decided against it. They had both been through a lot emotionally over the last twenty-four hours. It probably wouldn't be in their best interests to rush into making love right now. She thought about telling Max that they had already been lovers. No, there would be time for that later, too.

On returning to her desk after lunch on Monday, Deanna found a package waiting for her. Inside the gift-wrapped box she found a new swimsuit. It was a kelly-green one-piece suit—attractive, but very conservative in cut. Even before she opened the card, she knew who it was from. The bold male signature scrawled across the ivory paper confirmed her guess.

She called to thank him, but he was in a meeting. She left a message.

He returned her call later that afternoon. "Hi. Sorry I missed your call."

"I called to thank you for the new swimsuit."

"You're welcome. Would you like to break it in after work today?"

"Are you sure that's a good idea?"

"It will be lonely swimming laps without you," he coaxed. "Besides, your new swimsuit has two very sturdy shoulder straps and I've given up shark imitations."

She laughed. "Well . . . all right then."

That evening set the routine for the rest of the week. Every night at six-thirty, Max would knock at her door. Sometimes they went back to his apartment and swam, other times they stayed at Deanna's and played a game or watched TV. They always stayed far enough away from each other to avoid temptation, but Deanna would occasionally turn quickly and catch the flash of smoldering desire in Max's eyes as he watched her. She longed to beg him to let her down off the untouchable pedestal he'd placed her on, to be her lover as well as her friend.

On Thursday night, Max arrived on her door step carrying several brown bags. "I hope you like Chinese food."

"It looks like you bought out the whole restaurant, Max." Deanna laughed.

"I wasn't sure what you'd like."

Deanna went into the kitchen to get the plates and silverware, while Max started unpacking the bags.

* * *

After dinner they stored the leftovers in the refrigerator and set about washing up the dishes. Max was on drying detail. "By the way, I know it's a little late to ask, but am I trespassing on someone else's property?"

"What do you mean 'trespassing?' " Deanna rinsed out a glass and set it in the dish drainer.

"Well, it finally occurred to me that you might have been seriously involved with someone before I pushed my way into your life?"

"No, I haven't been seeing anyone on a regular basis. Would it make a difference if I was?"

"Not really, since we're just friends, but I feel less guilty monopolizing your time knowing there isn't some guy sitting home waiting for you." He hung the wet dish towel over the towel rack and then leaned back against the counter, his arms crossed over his chest. "You should have some guy sitting around waiting for you, though."

Deanna laughed and started into the living room.

Max followed. "I'm serious—a nice girl like you should find herself a good man to love, get married, and start a family."

"Max, I've been married." She sat down on one end of the couch.

Max eased himself down on the other end, angling his body to face hers. "The guy must have been a real idiot to let you go."

"I can see it that way now, but at the time I was

devastated. I took all the blame and responsibility for the failure on myself."

"What happened? If you don't mind my asking."

"I came home early from work one day and found him with another woman. Apparently, it had been going on for quite some time."

Max shook his head. "Now I know the guy was an idiot." He ran his hands down his thighs. "If you loved him, that must have been a dreadful experience."

"At the time, I loved him very much."

"Have you ever been in love with anyone else?"

Deanna hesitated before she spoke. "Once."

"Were you lovers?"

"Yes."

"What happened?"

Deanna swallowed. "It's a bit complicated."

"I've got time."

"I'd rather not talk about it."

Max looked hurt. "All right. Just one question. Was it before or after you were married?"

"After."

"Do you still see him?"

"That's two questions, Max."

Max shrugged and shook his head. "I just want to help. You looked rather wistful when I mentioned other lovers. I thought maybe I could do a little matchmaking and get the two of you back together."

What would he do if he knew that *he* was the other lover? Was this a good time to tell him?

Deanna thought back over the past week. They'd had a wonderful time together. The undercurrents of sexuality had finally settled down to a livable level. Did she want to stir them all up again?

She rubbed her chin thoughtfully. "I'm sure you'd look splendid in a loincloth with a quiver of arrows on your back, but I think you're a bit tall to be playing cupid."

"I just want you to be happy," Max insisted.

"I am happy," she assured him, truthfully. Being with him made her very happy. "What about you? Shall we try to marry you off, too?" she teased.

"I don't think so."

"Why? I'm sure we can find *someone* who's willing to put up with you." She flashed him a smile, a smile that Max didn't return.

"I don't always have regular hours. Sometimes I don't stop work until way after midnight. Sometimes I work all weekend. A wife needs more than I've got to give her."

"I think you're underestimating the woman you would fall in love with. She would love you for *all* that you are, including the dedicated businessman. Knowing how important your business is to you, she would be willing to work around your schedule just as you should be willing to work around any scheduling conflicts caused by her job or other interests."

"Even if the interests were other men?"

"Max!"

"I was sixteen years old the first time I was propositioned by a married woman and I told myself then, I would never get married."

"All right, granted some women's outside interest may lie in that direction, but not *all* married women go around propositioning other men. You shouldn't let the actions of a few women keep you from getting married."

"And not all men cheat on their wives so you shouldn't let that keep you from getting remarried!"

"That's not why I haven't remarried."

"It's not?" Max looked skeptical.

"It was at first, but . . ."

"Well, if that's not the reason now, then what is?"

"Now?" Deanna searched for a way to lighten the conversation. "Well, no one's asked, for one thing."

"And if someone did ask, would you marry him?" Max probed further.

"If I was in love with him."

"How would you know if you were in love?"

Deanna looked puzzled. "Haven't you ever been in love?"

"No, not that I remember."

Deanna's breath caught in her throat. Not that he remembered! It was the perfect opening to tell him, but the words stuck in her throat. If she told him about their love, would it scare him away? She quickly changed the subject. "So, how long have you had the cabin."

Max raised an eyebrow. "Rapid topic change, Deanna." His eyes narrowed.

"It's something I've been meaning to ask."

"I've had the cabin for the last five years. I needed someplace to get away by myself. Like a kid with a clubhouse or treehouse—someplace to take your friends, but not your parents. Someplace to hide when you need to think."

"Is that why you went up there after your argument with Alex."

"Yes, I needed to think. I was considering calling a halt to the resort chain."

"But the board voted to go along with the project."

"True, but Alex was against it. I respect his business opinion, and I was concerned that I might have hurt him. I was trying to imagine how I would feel if I had a son and he'd gone behind my back with a major project."

"There might be a little hurt involved, but I think you'd be proud of him, too. What had you decided to do before the accident?"

"I hadn't made a final decision. By the time I regained my memory, things were running full speed ahead." Max snapped his fingers. "I almost forgot. Tomorrow night Alex is having his annual Christmas party. It's for business associates, friends, and neighbors. Would you like to go?"

"Tomorrow night?"

"I know it's short notice, but with everything

that's been going on lately, it completely slipped my mind until Alex reminded me this afternoon. So what do you say, can I pick you up at seven-thirty?"

Deanna looked out the window as the limousine turned up the Hilliard driveway. The trees lining the way had been adorned with twinkling white lights for the occasion.

"How festive!" She turned to Max.

"Wait until you see what Vivian has done with the inside of the house," Max said.

"Vivian?"

"Alex's decorator. She decorates the house every year for the Christmas party. One year she had a portable ice-skating rink set up in the backyard, complete with figure skaters. Last year she had an underwater theme. The tree was made up of fans of turquoise coral. She draped it with garlands of pearls and hung shell-shaped iridescent ornaments."

"It sounds beautiful."

"It was. Not the least bit traditional, but it was beautiful. I like what she's done this year better."

"Well?" Deanna prompted.

"You'll just have to wait and see for yourself."

As the limousine pulled up to the front steps, an attendant opened the door and Max got out. He leaned back into the car to help Deanna. They walked up the steps together, Max's hand resting gently on the small of her back. Alex was standing in the entry hall greeting his guests.

After greeting Alex and meeting Vivian, who was hostess for the evening, Deanna and Max moved into the middle of the entry hall. Deanna looked around. Pine branches, pinecones, and traditional Christmas plaid with a touch of lace were incorporated into all the floral and decorative arrangements.

"Very traditional. I'm glad I wore a green dress."

"I'm glad you wore green, too." Max's eyes roamed over her in a visual caress. "Green is a good color for you."

"So you like the traditional Christmas look?" Deanna moved the conversation away from herself.

"I do. Maybe it's because my mother always decorated the house in green and red for Christmas. . . . Shall we get something to drink?"

Max led her past the stairway and through a set of open double doors. The party was in full swing. A buffet table stretched along the wall on one side of the room, and nearby were tables for diners. On the other end of the room was a bandstand, a dance floor, and plenty of room for mingling. In the center of the room was a Christmas tree. The bright star on top almost touched the ceiling. The traditional ornaments were over-size to match the tree's large proportions.

Max took two glasses of champagne from a passing waiter and gave one to Deanna. As they worked their way slowly through the crowd, he introduced her to many of the expensively dressed guests, most of whom were business associates and neighbors. By far the greater majority of the guests were closer in age to Alex than Max.

Deanna watched Max's cool, reserved, businesslike manner as he spoke with the guests. It was only briefly as they walked from group to group that a spark of mischief gleamed in his eyes and the corners of his lips threatened a more than polite smile.

When they reached the dance floor, Max took her into his arms. As they danced, he told her anecdotes about some of the people he'd introduced her to. Deanna was glad that he left a conservative space between them. She'd embarrassed herself once on a dance floor with him; she was in no hurry to do it again. Although she was in no danger of making a fool of herself in his arms, she was still painfully aware of the strong spell of physical attraction he had over her.

"Are you hungry?" Max asked, when the music stopped.

"N-not really." *Not for food anyway.*

Max tilted his head to one side. "Listen, I think I hear sleigh bells."

Max continued pretending to listen intently. "Sleigh bells *and* reindeer hoofs on the roof. Let's go see if Santa left anything for you under the Christmas tree." He took Deanna by the hand and started walking out of the ballroom.

"Max, the tree is right over there. Where are we going?"

"Santa wouldn't have been able to sneak anything

underneath that tree with all these people in here, silly." By this time they were back in the now-deserted entry hall. Max started up the stairs, still holding her hand.

They turned left at the top of the stairs. When they reached the end of the hallway, Max took a key ring out of his pocket and opened the door into his suite of rooms.

"Vivian?" Deanna asked as she indicated the decorated tree standing in the corner and the decorated fireplace mantel—complete with hanging stockings.

Max nodded as he walked over to the tree. He picked up a long flat package from underneath it. "I told you I heard Santa." He turned back to Deanna.

"Your gift is at home. If you had warned me I could have—"

"Just having you here is the most wonderful gift I can imagine," Max interrupted as he came to a stop before her and handed her the package, wrapped in green foil with a gold ribbon.

Deanna flipped open the attached gift card. Inside was written: "To My Best Friend. Love, Max." She closed the card as she looked up at Max. "Thank you," she said softly. She could feel the beginnings of tears forming in her eyes.

"No, thank *you*." He caressed her cheek. "Go ahead, open it."

"Why don't I save it until we get back to my apartment and you can open yours, too."

"No, I'd rather you opened it now."

Deanna carefully removed the bow and wrapping. As she suspected from the shape and feel of the package, there was a leather jewelry case inside. Opening the lid revealed a necklace of diamonds and emeralds. Her mouth opened, but no words came out.

"Do you like it?"

"It's beautiful, but—"

Max laughed. "No, buts. It's yours."

It *was* beautiful, but it probably cost more than her car, and she knew it cost much more than the blue sweater and pewter mammoth she'd bought for him. She didn't feel right accepting something so expensive.

Almost as though he were reading her mind, he said, "Don't put a price tag on it, Deanna. It's worth much less than what you've given me over the last week." He reached into the box and removed the necklace.

He turned her until her back was facing him. "I never considered the possibility of being this emotionally close to someone before," he continued as he stood behind her. "Most of the time I was too busy to even think about what I might be missing, and the rest of the time I just dismissed fulfilling interpersonal relationships as a myth."

He reached in front of her and placed the necklace on her. The gold and jewels felt cool against her chest, but the shiver that passed through her was caused by the light skimming of his warm fingers over her bare skin. She longed to lean back into him.

He gently moved her hair to one side as he closed the clasp. His fingers trailed across her back before he turned her to face him.

"Perfect," he appraised, although his eyes seemed to be focused slightly below the necklace.

Deanna blushed. "I don't know how to thank you."

"Just keep being here for me." He looked up.

"I will be." As long as he wanted her, she would be there. She loved him, and if a friend was what he needed, a friend was what she'd be to him—even though she longed for more.

Suddenly their surroundings seemed much too intimate. "I guess we'd better get back to the party," she said as she turned and started walking to the door. She was halfway there when Max called out her name. She stopped and turned toward him.

"Look." He pointed to the ceiling above her.

Deanna looked up. "Mistletoe?"

"Vivian never overlooks even the smallest detail. Bless her heart." He slowly crossed the room to stand in front of her. "May I—in the spirit of tradition?" He glanced up at the mistletoe.

Deanna's heart raced. There was nothing she wanted more at this moment than to have him kiss her. But would one kiss be enough?

ELEVEN

"Far be it for me to argue with tradition."

As his arms slid around her waist, hers moved up around his neck. Max pulled her in close to the hard length of his body. "It feels so good holding you in my arms," he murmured before he gently moved his lips onto hers.

As the familiar warmth and sensations spread through her, Deanna sighed. The slight parting of her lips was the opening Max had been waiting for. His tongue slipped in and teased her soft, sensitive inner lip before plunging deeply into the warm recesses of her mouth.

His hands moved up from her waist to wander over the skin left bare by the back of her dress. Tremors ran through her as she remembered the feel of his hands touching other parts of her body. Touches that could be soft and coaxing or strong and demanding.

She felt her breasts swell with longing and she moved them against the rock-hard wall of his chest, frustrated by the layers of clothing separating them.

Max moved his mouth off hers, trailing kisses down the side of her neck. His voice was a husky rasp as he told her, "I was afraid this would happen if I kissed you. I can't remember the last time I've ached this much wanting a woman." He straightened up, one hand curved gently around her neck as she tipped her head back to look up at him, and the other pushed against her lower back, moving her more tightly against his body. "Hell, I've *never* ached this much wanting a woman." With a groan, he took her mouth again.

Deanna knew what Max was feeling. She wanted him as much as he wanted her. Once again, the warm emotions of caring and friendship between them had flared up to become love and desire within her. "Love me, Max. I need you to love me," she whispered against his lips.

The solidness of the ground beneath her feet was swept away as he lifted her up in his arms, one arm behind her back and the other cradling her knees. He broke the kiss and looked down into her eyes. Could he see her passion there—as she could see his?

He carried her down the short hallway and into his bedroom. He stopped next to the bed. The soft glow of the bedside lamp illuminated only a small part of the spacious room. "Nervous?" he asked.

Deanna nodded. "A little." Her gaze dropped to his mouth, still wet from their kisses.

"Me, too." He smiled down at her.

She ran a finger along the curve of his cheek, ending up at his dimple. "*You*, nervous?"

He turned his head sideways. Capturing her finger with his teeth, he nibbled at it. With a last flick of his tongue, he released her finger.

"Satisfying you . . ." his hand slid down her back, taking the tab of her zipper with it, "is very important to me. I don't want you to be disappointed."

"I won't be." She helped him out of his jacket and tie, and went to work on his buttons.

Max slipped both hands into the back of her dress and slowly began to move it off her shoulders. "There is something beautiful and special between us, I don't want to lose that, but, on the other hand, something ignites inside me when you're near. I've been resisting it. . . . I can't anymore."

Deanna wasn't sure if he closed the distance between them or if she did, but once again they were locked in a hungry kiss. Deanna felt her dress slither down her body and fall to the floor.

She finished with Max's buttons and pushed open his shirt. Her moan echoed Max's when she molded herself against him. "I've dreamed of this since the day in the pool." He leaned down, running his tongue around one nipple before pulling it into his mouth.

Deanna's hands moved out to his suspenders, gripping them she slowly slid her hands down to where they were clipped to his pants. In no time at all she had them both unhooked. She sent his shirt to join her dress.

Max stood back up, looking deeply into her eyes. "I want you to know that, up until now, I'm the only person who has been in this bed."

Turning away, he pulled back the black-and-gray bedspread to reveal the soft black satin sheets underneath. In a combined effort, the collection of clothing on the floor grew larger. Deanna's Christmas gift was placed on the nightstand.

Max sat down on the edge of the bed, Deanna in his lap. He placed kisses along the curve of her breasts. He leaned back across the bed, drawing her with him.

She lay over him, her hair cascading down around his shoulders. He moved his legs so his thighs rested against the smooth sides of her hips. Her fingers moved through the dark hairs on his chest. She watched as his nipples tightened. Unable to resist the temptation, she moved her mouth over one nipple, imitating the motions Max had used earlier on her.

His hands, entwined in her hair, moved softly over the back of her head. When she lifted up, planning to move to the other side, he slid her forward and coaxed her mouth down over his.

Deanna felt herself sinking into a world of pure sensation. She could feel heat radiating from Max and the answering fire roaring up within her. All of the days and weeks that had gone by since they'd last made love seemed to fade away.

She rocked her hips lightly against his. Max growled deep in his throat before he reversed their positions by rolling her over onto her back. The smooth satin felt cool against her heated skin.

Max moved his lips off hers. He spread her hair out around her. "I knew you'd look beautiful on black satin. Almost too beautiful to touch." He ran his fingers down her cheek.

"I want you to touch me." Her voice was husky with desire. "Please touch me, Max."

His smile was slow and sensuous. "Oh, I intend to."

He kept his promise. His hands and lips created a myriad of luxurious sensations as they traveled over her body.

Deanna gasped his name out loud as he moved over her, joining them together. At first he lay still against her. She opened her eyes and found him watching her.

"Perfect," he whispered before he leaned down and kissed her deeply. Max groaned as Deanna gently pulled his tongue into her mouth. He slid his hands down her sides and underneath her hips to pull her more tightly against him as be began moving within her.

The magic was there again, as she'd relived it in her mind countless times. She gave herself up to it, forgetting everything but the reality of the man in her arms.

As waves of pleasure crashed through her, she could faintly hear Max's voice. She couldn't make out the words, but she could sense the intense emotions behind them. She ran her hands down across his back as she felt him join her in release.

Deanna's heart and breathing rates slowly returned to normal. Max rolled them back over, keeping her on top of him. She laid her head down, pillowed on his chest.

"And you were nervous," Max teased.

Deanna laughed. "So were you," she reminded him.

"I told you why I was nervous. Why were you nervous?" he asked.

"Just feeling insecure, I guess. Not sure that I'd be able to measure up."

"Well, you can put your fears to rest. You are one incredible lady." He kissed the top of her head and held her close as they both drifted off into a contented sleep.

Several hours later, Deanna woke to find Max sitting on the side of the bed with a tray with two full plates. He was wearing his bathrobe.

"I hope you didn't go through the buffet line in your bathrobe."

He smiled down at her. "I had Mark fix the tray and then bring it up before I sent him home. We won't be needing him anymore tonight, will we?"

"You want me to stay?"

"I want you to stay."

"All night?"

"All weekend."

They spent the rest of the weekend in Max's suite. They had everything they needed—a small but well stocked kitchen and each other.

Saturday morning Max had a few items of business to take care of. He had a small office next to the kitchen in his suite. Max sat down at the computer terminal in his bathrobe. Deanna, wearing one of Max's shirts, curled up on the couch. She had picked a book off the bookshelf and was soon involved in the hero's quest to save the world from terrorists.

She didn't realize Max had finished his work until she heard him reading over her shoulder, " 'Taking Nicole by the hand, Ted headed for the bedroom.' " Max reached down and took her hand. "I think Ted's got a great idea. Shall we?"

"Max, Ted and Nicole haven't seen each other in six months. We just made love an hour ago."

"An hour?"

"Approximately."

Max looked down at his watch, counting quietly to himself. "Now." He came around to the front of the couch, sweeping her up into his arms. "It's approximately an hour and thirty seconds and I want you again. Any objections?"

"None."

As with all good things, it ended much too soon and they had to return to the rest of the world. Deanna decided this must be how a butterfly feels when it crawls out of its cocoon—new, beautiful, excited that the best stage of its life is beginning.

Monday morning, Max drove her back to her apartment. She was wearing one of his sweatsuits. It was big on her, but the elastic in the wrists and ankles helped.

She stood in the living room and looked around. "It seems like I've been away for years."

"It *does* feel like it's been more than two days." Max came up behind her and drew her back against him. "I'm going to miss you today. I'll be counting the hours until six-thirty."

They continued to see each other every day after work, except now, instead of long talks across a table or sitting side by side on the couch, they talked wrapped in each other's arms, heads side by side on the pillow.

Wednesday night they went out to dinner with Glen and Kathy. It was the first time they'd gone out together since their physical relationship had resumed. It was hard sitting next to him at the table and not being free to touch or kiss him where or when she felt like it. From the fires burning in Max's eyes, she could see that he was finding it uncomfortable, also.

During coffee, Kathy excused herself from the table. Deanna joined her.

Instead of going back to the table immediately, Kathy sat down on one of the couches in the ladies' lounge.

"I can't believe the change in Max. We've known him a long time and I've never seen him so relaxed and happy. He's always been so cold and reserved. He's a whole new person. It's amazing." Kathy slipped off her shoes. "I've got to get out of these heels for a few minutes."

Deanna sat down next to her.

"I'm not the only one who's noticed the change," Kathy continued. "Audrey's seen the difference, too."

"Your daughter Audrey?"

"Yes. I couldn't believe it when I came into the living room this evening and found her sitting in Max's lap."

"She came right over to him the minute we sat down."

"She does that to many people, but never with Max! She's always watched him cautiously, but hasn't gone to him, even if he's called her."

"Maybe she's just getting used to him," Deanna suggested.

"No, he's changed and she senses it. I think it's

wonderful." She slipped her shoes back on. "Guess we'd better head back before the guys come looking for us."

"From the looks of things, you could have given your feet a longer rest," Deanna remarked tightly as she looked across the room toward their table.

"No, if we waited any longer Glen would be drooling so hard he'd drown half the people in here."

Jennifer Brady was sitting in Deanna's chair, wearing a flashy low-cut silver evening dress. As they watched she laughed at something Glen said and leaned toward Max as she wrapped her arm around his, angling herself to give him a full view down the front of her dress.

"I'll bet she practices that move in the mirror," Kathy muttered. "Come on, Deanna, let's go."

Deanna didn't feel like going to the table. She wanted to curl up into a little ball somewhere. She felt a dull, numbing ache in her chest—much like the ache she'd felt when she'd walked in on Kevin.

"Hey, are you all right?" Kathy's voice cut through the fog in her mind.

"I'm fine," Deanna answered tightly.

"You don't look fine, you're white as a ghost." Kathy put her hand on Deanna's upper arm. "You're not worried about that bit of Hollywood fluff are you?"

Deanna shrugged, her eyes never leaving the scene across the room from them.

"Look at Max closely, Deanna," Kathy demanded, giving her arm a squeeze. "She might as well be a spot on the wall for all the attention he's paying to her. On the other hand, Glen, that skunk, is making a fool of himself."

Kathy was right, but Deanna was still unable to shake her disquiet.

"Come on." Kathy prodded her gently.

Deanna was surprised to find that her feet followed orders and actually moved her forward. As they got closer to the table, Deanna kept her eyes on Max, watching his every move, every expression on his face. He was wearing his cold, aloof facade; until he looked up and saw them approaching.

He smiled at her and her fears dissolved. The coolness had left his features. Whatever had been between him and Jennifer was over. She felt something click inside. It was as if her alarm clock had gone off, but instead of opening her eyes to find her dream disappearing with the morning light, he was still there waiting. It was hard for her to believe, but she was beginning to trust him.

The joy of it was overpowering. Kevin had robbed her of her ability to trust. Max was giving it back to her.

When they arrived, the men stood up. Max put his arm around Deanna's shoulder, holding her close by his side. Glen handled the introductions.

Jennifer coolly acknowledged Kathy. When she was introduced to Deanna, she was downright frosty.

Jennifer rose. "I'd better get back to my guests."
She was looking thoughtfully at Deanna. "Have we
met before? You look familiar."

"No, we've never met," Deanna fibbed, confident
that Jennifer would have forgotten all about her
masquerading as a freelance writer.

"Well, I meet *so* many people. It's been a pleasure meeting you, Glen." She flashed him a smile.
"And you ladies, too," she added as an afterthought.
"Max, dear, you've got my number." She brushed
a kiss across his cheek.

"We've all got *her* number," Kathy whispered
under her breath to Deanna.

Deanna fought back the urge to laugh. The four
of them sat back down at the table.

"Max, dear," Kathy said, in a perfect imitation
of Jennifer, "you have lipstick on your cheek."

Max picked up his napkin and handed it to
Deanna. He turned his face up, cheek toward her.
She rubbed the red stain off with the cloth, then ran
her bare fingers over his warm skin. "Good as
new," she told him.

"Thanks," his voice was tight, strained, and the
desire in his eyes told her more than words how her
small touch had affected him.

Glen must have noticed, also. "Well, gang. Shall
we call it a night?"

On Thursday evening she arrived at Max's apartment to find a Christmas tree standing in the corner

of the living room and a row of shopping bags lined up in front of the unlit fireplace. She walked over and peeked in the first one. "Ornaments?"

"Right. I've never had a tree here at the apartment, so I picked up a few things to decorate it with."

"A few things?" Deanna laughed. "Max, there's enough here for three trees!"

"Really?"

Deanna nodded.

"So, pick what you want to use this year and we'll pack the rest away for another Christmas."

Another Christmas? It was the first time he'd mentioned the future. Had he meant there would be another Christmas for them or would someone else be here with him next year? She wished she had the courage to ask exactly what he'd meant, but she didn't want to jeopardize the happiness of the moment.

Her new-found trust kept her from suspecting he would be unfaithful to her while their relationship lasted, but how long would it last? He'd given her no signs. He hadn't even told her he loved her; although she could see it in his eyes and feel it in his touch.

Max dug through one of the bags. "Ta-da," he announced as he held up the packages of lights. "It's been a long time since I've decorated a Christmas tree myself, but I do remember that the lights go first."

In no time at all, the brightly twinkling lights were

draped around the tree's branches. Next, they sorted through the other bags choosing ornaments. It took an hour to decorate the tree. Max put the ornaments on the upper branches. Deanna worked on the lower branches. When he finished, Max stood to the side watching her quietly.

"Done." She stepped back to look. Going to the tree, she shifted one of the ornaments a few inches to the left, another to the right. "Okay, turn out the lights."

Max didn't say anything as he walked over and turned off the living room lights.

"What do you think?" Deanna asked.

"I think it's perfect and if you touch one more ornament, you'll ruin it."

Deanna looked at him over her shoulder, a smile tugging at the corner of her mouth. "Really?"

Max nodded. "I also think it's time we scouted through the rest of the bags for the mistletoe."

"Mistletoe? You bought mistletoe?"

"I did."

"Do you think we need it?"

"Will you kiss me without it?"

Deanna looked back at the Christmas tree, then turned to face Max. "I might."

Max laughed. "You might? That's encouraging."

The ringing of the telephone intruded on their privacy. Max looked at his watch before moving over to the phone on the end table. By the time he picked it up, the laughter was gone and he was one hundred percent businessman.

The conversation was short and Deanna couldn't make heads or tails of it, only hearing Max's side. But she could see by his face and stance, whatever was being said displeased him.

After hanging up, he asked, "How would you like to go to Phoenix for a few days?"

"Phoenix, Arizona?"

"Yes. We've started the first resort and there have been a few problems. I've been trying to handle things by phone, but . . ."

Deanna wanted to say yes, but since she'd given up working overtime, she'd decided to accept Gordon's offer to hire an assistant. She had interviews scattered over the next few days.

"I'd like to go with you, Max, but I can't get away from work right now."

"Can't someone cover for you?"

"Normally it wouldn't be a big problem, but I'm interviewing for an assistant and that's not something I can delegate."

"I understand." He came over to her, taking her into his arms. "Maybe next time."

"Next time," she agreed.

"What am I going to do in Phoenix without you?"

"Max, you'll be working."

"Right. These troubleshooting trips involve long hours of work and falling into bed exhausted at the end of the day." He cuddled her closely against his chest. "I'm going to miss holding you at night."

"I'm going to miss being held."

"Guess I'll just have to squeeze my pillow."

Deanna hoped he wouldn't forget his plans and find *someone* in place of his pillow. This trip would certainly put her new-found trust to the test.

TWELVE

He was only gone one week, but it seemed like forever.

She found her assistant on the third day of interviews. In her now free evenings she cleaned her apartment, caught up on the laundry, addressed Christmas cards, went over to her mother's to help bake Christmas cookies, finished up her Christmas shopping, and through it all missed Max.

On the day he was due back, Deanna tried to stay calm and collected as she rode the elevator up to his apartment, but she was a bundle of nerves.

He'd called her every day while he was away, but over the last few days he'd started sounding more remote. Had he just been preoccupied with his work or was his interest starting to wane? They hadn't been together very long, but in comparison to Max's track record . . .

She'd tried telling herself that it was just her old insecurities flaring up again and not to worry, but the uneasiness continued. She told herself it was silly to suspect that he might be seeing other women, but she still couldn't help wondering.

She remembered what Kevin had said to her as she'd packed her bags, "There's no need for you to leave. I still love you. Men need a little variety, that's all. There are so many ready, willing women around and I'm certainly able."

Was he right? Did men need variety? Did Max? He'd had variety in the past, was it realistic to expect him to give it up?

Her thoughts were interrupted as the elevator door slid open. Stepping out, she was immediately swept into Max's arms.

"I missed you," he whispered against her lips, before his mouth came down fully onto hers in an urgent kiss. A kiss that she eagerly returned. How could she have doubted him, even for a minute?

His hands moved slowly up her sides and across her back. He lifted his head, looking down at her, his eyes blazing.

"Welcome home," Deanna whispered.

"It's good to be home." He ran his hand down the side of her cheek before turning back toward the apartment. He tucked her tightly against his side as the two of them entered the front door.

As Max headed in the direction of the hallway leading to his bedroom, the housekeeper appeared. "Baxter says that dinner is ready, Mr. Hilliard."

"Thank you, Mrs. Evans. We'll be right there."

"Very good, sir."

After Mrs. Evans made her exit, Max turned to Deanna. "Well, shall we run the risk of offending Baxter and shocking Mrs. Evans or shall we go into the dining room?"

Deanna ran her tongue along her bottom lip. "We'd better go into the dining room."

From the minute they entered the dining room, Deanna wished she'd chosen differently. She recognized the soft classical music at once. The candlelit table for two added to the eerie déjà vu feeling. She took several steps into the room, but stopped shortly when she saw the centerpiece—silver candleholders surrounded by red roses lying on a bed of pine along with several pinecones. There hadn't been any roses in Montana, but the concept was the same.

She didn't hear a word Max said as he walked her to the table. He pulled her chair out for her. She sat down slowly. She ran her hand over the handle of the silver knife, down the cool stem of the crystal wineglass, over the ivory linen napkin—remembering.

Max poured the wine. "I'd like to make a toast." He lifted his wineglass. "To us."

Had he really said it or was she hearing echoes from the past? Deanna touched the side of her glass to his, took a small sip, and then set her glass down.

Max gave her a puzzled look. "Deanna, are you all right?"

"I'm fine," she lied. "Tell me about Phoenix." Max talked about his trip. Deanna listened only well enough to make the correct responses.

Her mind was a whirlpool of questions. Had he remembered everything? Was he waiting for her to comment? Was it just a coincidence? A cold rush of fear washed over her as yet another possibility came into her thoughts. Was Max playing cruel games with her?

She'd let all her defenses down again and let him back into her heart over the past few weeks. If he'd remembered everything, could he have set out to win her love and then throw it back at her as revenge for her leaving him in Montana?

Part of her cried out that she couldn't have misjudged him, but another part reminded her how poor her judgment about men typically was. Hadn't he told her in the beginning that he was a rake and rat? She had trusted her father and Kevin, and they'd let her down. Was she wrong to have trusted Max? Had she fallen into the same trap again?

Deanna was not the least bit surprised when the main course turned out to be Beef Bourguignon, served with rice and broccoli.

"Mr. Hilliard." Mrs. Evans came into the dining room. "Mr. Jacobs is on the phone from London. Would you like to take the call?"

"I've been trying to reach him. Deanna, would you mind? It shouldn't take too long."

"No, go right ahead."

Max ran his hand across her back in a gentle caress on his way out of the room. Not at all what one would expect from someone cold and calculating, getting ready to go in for the kill.

Once she was alone, she gave up pretending to eat. She got up and wandered into the living room. The only light came from the twinkling lights on the Christmas tree and candles that were placed around the room. Tonight the floor-to-ceiling drapes were pulled back to reveal a wall of windows with a wide, cushioned ledge.

She curled up on one of the window-seat cushions. The simple act of curling her knees up underneath her seemed to relieve part of the heavy weight around her heart. She pulled back the silky sheer curtain that covered the window. It felt cool in her hands.

She looked out across the glittering lights of the city. The L.A. skyline looked different when you were in the middle of it. The lights were beautiful in their own way, but couldn't compare with the black, starlit night sky of Montana.

She watched the cars move silently down the street many stories below her. Someone came out of the building across the street and hopped into a waiting car.

Her mind slipped back in time to the night she and Max had stood on the balcony and watched the northern lights together. The night they had declared their love for each other. The night he had come to her room and made love to her.

The lights of the city sparkled with crystalline brilliance as she watched them from behind a veil of tears. She lay her forehead against the cool glass.

She didn't hear Max call her name. She didn't even realize that he had entered the room until he came up behind her and placed his hand on her hip.

Kneading her hipbone gently, he leaned over and placed a kiss on the side of her neck. "For a minute there, I was afraid you'd gone home." He sat down next to her and slowly turned her to face him. His smile faded when he saw her tears. Wordlessly, he gathered her close against his chest, running his hands across her back and through her hair.

Deanna was torn between wanting to pull away and demand the truth and wanting to forget everything but the feel of him.

For a long while he just held her as she cried. Finally he asked, "Do you want to talk about it?"

"I'm not sure."

"Does it have something to do with me?"

She leaned back until she had a clear view of his face. "Have you remembered the weeks you had amnesia?" She held her breath as she waited for his answer.

A look of genuine confusion passed over Max's face. He shook his head. "What makes you think I've remembered anything?"

"Dinner . . . the centerpiece . . . the music . . ."

"What about dinner, the centerpiece, and the music? Could you be more specific?"

Max looked even more puzzled, and in a flash Deanna knew that he really had no idea what she was talking about. The tears started again. She put her arms around his neck and pulled him close. "You don't remember. This wasn't your way of trying to hurt me."

"Hurt you?" Max pulled back until he could look down into her face. "How can you even suspect that I would ever do anything to hurt you?"

"I . . ." Looking into his eyes, Deanna could see the hurt her suspicions had caused. "Maybe I should start at the beginning. . . ."

Nestled in his arms, she told him the whole story. Starting with the way she had felt the first time his eyes had met hers across the hospital lounge. She described the spell he had cast over her with their first kiss. She told him how she had tried to discourage him by pretending that they were separated and how he had set out to win her back. She told him about Chez Max, matching item to item with their dinner tonight.

"Bourguignon is one of Baxter's specialties. He's the one who fixed dinner tonight. I left the menu entirely in his hands. I have the recipe in a cookbook that he made up for me that I keep at the cabin," he explained. "As for the centerpiece, either Baxter or Mrs. Evans ordered it, I don't even know which."

He ran his hands through her hair. "I picked the music, because it happens to be one of my favorites and yes, I think I do also have this tape up at the cabin."

"So, all the similarities are just a coincidence?"

"Apparently. That's not the end of the story, though, is it?"

Deanna continued recounting the events in Montana: the northern lights, their declarations of love, Max's decision not to make love to her, his coming in to her room and the brief passion-filled hours.

"That other guy you told me about, the one you were in love with after your divorce . . . it was me wasn't it?"

"Yes."

Max sighed. "Is it possible to be jealous of yourself? God, I wish I could remember our falling in love the first time. You can't imagine how much it frustrates me to have lost that."

Deanna hugged him. "I think the memories are there somewhere inside you."

"When I regained my memory, why didn't you tell me about our relationship?"

"At that point there wasn't much of a relationship to tell you about."

"What happened to separate us?"

"When Alex and Dr. Fletcher arrived, I felt guilty about what had happened."

"Why? We were two consenting adults."

"True, but you thought we were married. I felt

guilty about having deceived you." She caught her bottom lip between her teeth.

"But you were following doctor's orders, right?"

"Yes, but it still felt wrong." She sighed. "Plus, I was worried about what would happen when you got your memory back. I was afraid you wouldn't want me anymore."

"But I'd told you that I loved you," Max reminded her.

"I know, but you thought we were married."

"I don't think that's enough to make someone feel love for someone else. If I told you that I loved you, I'm sure that's what I was feeling."

"It sounds logical now, but at the time I felt very awkward and very afraid." She looked down at his chest, unable to look him in the eyes as she continued. "So afraid, that when you found out we weren't really married, I let you think I was still married to Kevin."

"Why?"

"So you would let me go."

"You wanted to leave me?"

"Not really. But I couldn't face the thought of you leaving me once you regained your memory. It hurt me to leave you, but at the time I thought it would be easier than waiting for you to leave me."

Max put his hands along the sides of her face and tilted her head back until she was looking him in the eyes. "Didn't it occur to you that we might have stayed together once my memory returned?"

"What chance did I have?" Her voice broke. "I had one disastrous marriage behind me and you had a black book the size of the Los Angeles phone book."

As the tears began again, Max gently wiped them away. "All of those numbers were just part of the search. At the time I didn't even know what I was searching for. Now that I've found you, I don't need the others."

"Not even for variety?"

"Variety?" Max laughed. "I've got plenty of variety. You—morning, afternoon, evening, spring, summer, fall, winter. The bed, the couch, the hot tub. Do I need to continue?"

Deanna shook her head.

"What happened next?"

"I left you at the cabin with your father and Dr. Fletcher. After you came back, you somehow found out about the divorce. Understandably, you were angry that I hadn't told you the truth in Montana. We argued. I . . . I went away for the weekend. There was a message from you on my answering machine when I got home."

"The message that you tried to answer the day my memory returned," Max guessed correctly.

"When I heard your message, I hoped and prayed that you were willing to forgive me and give us another chance. When Tracy buzzed me to say that Mr. Hilliard was on the phone, I thought it was you. But it was Alex asking me to come to the hospital."

"And you arrived, expecting to find a lover and found a stranger instead."

Deanna nodded.

"Sweet Deanna." Max pulled her tightly into his arms. "We've had a rough time of it, haven't we?"

He nuzzled the side of her neck until she turned her head and pressed her open mouth to his. It was a kiss to heal all of the old wounds, to erase all of the bad memories, to wipe the slate clean.

Without breaking the kiss, Max shifted her to one side. She felt him reach into his jacket. He slowly moved back, placing several light kisses on her lips before sitting all the way up.

Silently, he held his hand out between them, a small leather box in the middle of his palm. Deanna looked at the box and then at Max.

"I told you once that you should find yourself a good man to love, get married, settle down, and start a family. The last few days I've done a lot of soul-searching and I've decided that *I* want to be that man, Deanna."

He flipped open the box. The diamond solitaire ring sparkled in the candlelight. "It was all there for me from the beginning, but I didn't recognize it. Wanting to be with you whenever possible, needing to share thoughts and feelings with you, and despite all my best efforts to ignore it—wanting and needing to make love to you." He removed the ring from its case.

Taking a deep breath, he continued. "Hell . . . what I'm trying to say is that I love you."

Deanna rested her hands on the sides of his neck. "I love you, too."

Max smiled. He took her left hand in his, the heat of his palm radiating into hers. Holding the ring at the end of her finger, he asked, "May I?"

"Please."

He kissed her again—a kiss full of promises for the future.

Deanna looked at the ring on her finger. "I can't believe this. The last few days, you seemed preoccupied on the phone. I had begun to think you were going to say you wanted to see other people."

"I bought the ring a few days ago, but I wanted to wait and ask you to marry me in person. I'm sorry if I frightened you. I was trying to keep from spoiling the surprise."

"It's beautiful."

"Well, soon-to-be-Mrs. Maxwell Hilliard, shall we head back to the dining room and finish dinner?"

"It seems to me that we have some other unfinished business left over from before dinner. . . ." Her eyes focused on the hallway leading to the master bedroom as she ran her fingers down the row of buttons on his shirt.

"Yes, I remember. We didn't want to shock the staff." His hands moved to the sides of her breasts, his thumbs coming around to make slow, lazy circles over her nipples.

"Right."

"I sent them home."

"You sent them home?"

Max nodded slowly. "About that unfinished business . . ."

Deanna reached up to the knot of his tie. "I'm ready anytime you are."

SHARE THE FUN . . .
SHARE YOUR NEW-FOUND TREASURE!!

You don't want to let your new books out of your sight? That's okay. Your friends can get their own. Order below.

No. 17 OPENING ACT by Ann Patrick
The summer really heats up when big city playwright meets small town sheriff.

No. 18 RAINBOW WISHES by Jacqueline Case
Mason is looking for more from life. Evie may be his pot of gold!

No. 19 SUNDAY DRIVER by Valerie Kane
Carrie breaks through all Cam's defenses and shows him how to love.

No. 20 CHEATED HEARTS by Karen Lawton Barrett
T.C. and Lucas find their way back into each other's hearts.

No. 21 THAT JAMES BOY by Lois Faye Dyer
Jesse believes in love at first sight. Now he has to convince Sarah of this.

No. 22 NEVER LET GO by Laura Phillips
Ryan has a big dilemma and Kelly is the answer to *all* his prayers.

No. 23 A PERFECT MATCH by Susan Combs
Ross can keep Emily safe but can he save himself from Emily?

No. 24 REMEMBER MY LOVE by Pamela Macaluso
Will Max ever remember the special love he and Deanna shared?

Kismet Romances
Dept 1290, P. O. Box 41820, Philadelphia, PA 19101-9828

Please send the books I've indicated below. Check or money order only—no cash, stamps or C.O.D.'s (PA residents, add 6% sales tax). I am enclosing $2.75 plus 75¢ handling fee for *each* book ordered.
Total Amount Enclosed: $_____.

____ No. 17   ____ No. 19   ____ No. 21   ____ No. 23
____ No. 18   ____ No. 20   ____ No. 22   ____ No. 24

Please Print:
Name_____
Address_____Apt. No._____
City/State_____ Zip_____

Allow four to six weeks for delivery. Quantities limited.

Kismet Romances has for sale a Mini Handi Light to help you when reading in bed, reading maps in the car, or for emergencies where light is needed. Features an on/off switch; lightweight plastic housing and strong-hold clamp that attaches easily to books, car visor, shirt pocket, etc. 11″ long. Requires 2 "AA" batteries (not included). If you would like to order, send $9.95 each to: Mini Handi Light Offer, P.O. Box 41820, Phila., PA 19101-9828. PA residents must add 6% sales tax. Please allow 8 weeks for delivery. Supplies are limited.